"Don't try to figure me out, Autumn," Campbell said.

"I'm just a man who was lost once. Now I've found my way. I only ask that you don't push me away, because I need to be here, right here, working for your father."

Autumn sighed. Did he think she was fishing for information just so she could report back to her father and push Campbell out of business? Did he really think she was that ruthless?

"I wasn't planning on shoving you out the door," she said, a little spark of anger replacing her need to nurture him. "I just wanted to know more about you."

"Well, now you do," he said, gently taking her arm and leading her into the restaurant. He stopped at the door. "Oh, and I promised your father I wouldn't ever hurt you."

"I don't think we need to worry about that."

"No, but I didn't exactly promise him I wouldn't fall for you, either. Because that's a promise I don't think I'm going to be able to keep."

Books by Lenora Worth

Love Inspired

The Wedding Quilt #12
Logan's Child #26
I'll Be Home for Christmas #44
Wedding at Wildwood #53
His Brother's Wife #82
Ben's Bundle of Joy #99
The Reluctant Hero #108
One Golden Christmas #122
**When Love Came to Town* #142
**Something Beautiful* #169
**Lacey's Retreat* #184
†*The Carpenter's Wife* #211
†*Heart of Stone* #227
†*A Tender Touch* #269
A Certain Hope #311
A Perfect Love #330
A Leap of Faith #344

Steeple Hill

After the Storm
Echoes of Danger

**In the Garden
†Sunset Island
*Texas Hearts

LENORA WORTH

knew she wanted to be a writer after her fourth-grade teacher assigned a creative writing project. While the other children moaned and groaned, Lenora gleefully wrote her first story, then promptly sold it (for a quarter) on the playground. She actually started selling in bookstores in 1993. Before joining Steeple Hill, Lenora wrote for Avalon and Leisure Books.

Married for thirty years, Lenora has two children. Before writing full-time, she worked in marketing and public relations. She has served in her local RWA chapter and as president of Faith, Hope, and Love, the inspirational chapter of RWA. She also wrote a weekly opinion column for the *Shreveport Times* for five years, and now writes a monthly column for *SB* magazine.

A LEAP OF FAITH
LENORA WORTH

Steeple Hill®

Published by Steeple Hill Books™

STEEPLE HILL BOOKS

**Steeple
Hill®**

ISBN 0-373-81258-2

A LEAP OF FAITH

Copyright © 2006 by Lenora H. Nazworth

This edition published by arrangement with Steeple Hill Books.

® and TM are trademarks of Steeple Hill Books, used under license.
Trademarks indicated with ® are registered in the United States Patent
and Trademark Office, the Canadian Trade Marks Office and in other
countries.

www.SteepleHill.com

Printed in U.S.A.

By faith we understand that the worlds were framed by the word of God, so that the things which are seen were not made of things which are visible.

—*Hebrews* 11:3

To my fellow Love Inspired authors—
friends, sisters and awesome writers all!

Chapter One

"Weddings always make me cry."

Autumn Maxwell turned to the tall, dark-haired man who'd just whispered that slightly sarcastic statement, apparently for her ears only. He wasn't what she'd call handsome. But he wasn't hard to look at, either. He had brown, almost black eyes and hair about the same color. He wore an impeccably tailored gray lightweight suit with dark gray suede lace-up shoes that could only be described as sneakers.

Wondering why he'd decided to bother *her,* Autumn gave him a once-over then said, "I don't see any tears."

He slanted his head sideways, causing his thick hair to ruffle across his forehead, then held a hand to his heart. "In here. I'm crying in here."

"Oh, well, that explains it then." Autumn tuned out his pleasant drawling accent, then turned to stare out at the crowd of people mingling by the shimmering swimming pool at the Big M Ranch in Paris, Texas.

They were celebrating the wedding of Autumn's cousin, April Maxwell, to Reed Garrison. Reed had been April's high school sweetheart and the man she'd fallen in love with all over again when she'd come home earlier this year. Autumn knew this had been an emotional day for April. Her father, Stuart, had passed away back in the spring, and her mother had died years ago in a plane crash. But today, April looked joyful as she mingled with her guests in the soft late-September sunshine. She loved Reed, and they were happy together at last, in spite of how much April missed her parents. April and Reed had a strong faith that would see them through. And they'd have a good marriage. Autumn sent up thanks for that, even while her own heart hurt with loneliness.

"Explains what?" the man beside Autumn asked, leaning toward her, his broad shoulders blocking her view.

Autumn looked up at him, a tired kind of reluctance pulling at her very bones as she refocused on him. Giving him a weak smile, she asked, "Are you still here?"

"Ouch, that hurt." He grinned then extended a hand. "Campbell Dupree, *invited* guest."

Autumn took his hand, shook it, then drew back, the jolt of awareness his touch had brought knocking her off balance for only an instant. "Autumn Maxwell, *cousin of the bride.*"

He stood straight up, his eyebrows slanting as he grinned. "I know who you are."

That smug admission caused Autumn to step back. She didn't like the intimate way he was looking at her. "And *how* do you know who I am?"

He drew his head back, his eyes locked on her face. "I saw you in the wedding party, but I had no idea—"

"Second bridesmaid to the left," Autumn retorted, a wry smile on her face.

His gaze moved over her face. "As I was trying to explain, I was told before the wedding that you and your cousin Summer would be attendants, but I had no idea how pretty you'd both be. Especially you."

Autumn let out a laugh. "Okay, you should just can the sweet talk. We all know Summer is the pretty one. April is the stylish one, and me, well, I'm the plain one."

He shook his head. "Depends on your definition of plain. Right now, you don't look plain at all. You look radiant."

She hid her unladylike snort behind her hand. "Are you for real?"

He looked down at himself, patted his chest and shoulders. "I feel real."

Autumn could attest to that. He looked solid, as if he worked out on a regular basis. Nice biceps aside, she really wished he'd just go away. She wanted to stand here and enjoy watching April and Reed laughing with their guests. This was their day, so Autumn refused to think any negative thoughts. Except this annoying man with the strange shoes and the dark, mysterious eyes was making that difficult.

"Is there something else you'd like to say?" she asked the man, since he was still watching, make that *ogling* her.

"So you're Richard Maxwell's daughter?"

She mimicked his earlier moves, slapping her hands against her bare arms. "Yes, last time I checked." Then she made a face to discourage any more questions. "And it was really nice to meet you, but I'm going to walk away now, okay?"

"Why?" He followed her back toward the punch table on the long patio of the Big M's ranch house. "Why are you walking away?"

Autumn fingered the delicate strand of pearls April had given her for being a bridesmaid, then pushed at the smooth chignon she'd been forced to endure in order to please the bride's sense of style.

"Because I'm not a very social person, and because you're beginning to get on my last nerve."

He stepped in front of the punch bowl, a beseeching grin splitting his face. "But you hardly know me."

"My point exactly," Autumn said, trying to scoot around him. Suddenly, she was very thirsty and that almond tea punch was looking better and better.

Campbell Dupree headed her off by coming around to the back of the table. He stood staring over the crystal bowl at her while he ladled her some punch. Handing her the cup, he asked, "So you attend weddings, even participate in them, but you don't enjoy being around other people at the receptions?"

"Something like that," Autumn replied, her smile practiced and efficient. She downed the whole cup of punch, hoping he'd be gone by the time she got to the bottom.

He wasn't.

"And just why *aren't* you a social person?"

Giving him a shrug of impatience that caused her blush-colored sleeveless bridesmaid dress to shimmer, she replied, "I deal in numbers. I'm an accountant. Or at least I was."

"In New York," he said, admiration flickering in his eyes. "I've heard all about that."

"You have?" Curious now, Autumn stopped thinking about how to get away. "How do you know all about me? Are you one of my father's clients or business buddies, or are you a friend of Reed's?"

Before he could answer, her father came barreling up to them. "There you are," he said to Autumn. "I've been looking for you. I see you've met Campbell."

"Yes," Autumn said, wondering with renewed interest how her father knew Campbell Dupree, and wondering why her father seemed so nervous and flushed. "He was just about to tell me—"

"I was just about to tell her yet again how very lovely she looks," Campbell said, his smoky gaze moving from her father to Autumn. "As I said earlier, you and your cousin make a lovely pair of bridesmaids."

"Thanks," Autumn said, thinking the man was surely repetitive and just a bit too charming. Glancing back at her perspiring father she asked, "Daddy, are you okay?"

Richard Maxwell looked as handsome as ever in his dark suit and shiny cowboy boots, but a fine sheen of moisture glowed across his forehead. "I'm fine, honey. But we need to talk. In private."

"Is something wrong?" Autumn said, glancing around. "Is April okay?"

"April is one happy bride," Richard replied. "And Summer is inside with little Michael. Poor little fellow—tough about him losing his mother last month. But Summer and Mack are doing a fine job of surrounding him with love. I reckon they'll be having their own wedding soon."

Autumn nodded. Her father was sand-bagging for some reason. Apparently, he had something he really wanted to say, but he was talking about everything but that, whatever it was.

She watched as his glance bounced back and forth between Campbell Dupree and her. "What's the matter, Daddy?"

"Let's go inside," Richard said, giving Campbell a warning look. "You don't mind, do you?"

"Not at all, sir," Campbell said, backing away. "It was nice to meet you, Autumn."

"You, too," Autumn said, not exactly sure if the word *nice* would describe this particular meeting.

She did need to talk to her father, however. Wondering how she was going to break the news that her company in New York had downsized and she'd been laid off, Autumn followed Richard into the cool interior of the house. She'd arrived home for the wedding three days ago, but she hadn't been able to find the right time to tell her father that she might have to move back to Atlanta, Texas, and work at his financial firm for a while. Just until she could figure out what to do with the rest of her life.

Maybe this layoff had been a blessing in disguise. April was now married and back at the Big M. Summer had moved back to Athens, Texas, to work as a counselor at the Golden Vista Retirement Village, and to be with her new love, Mack Riley. That had left Autumn all alone in New York. All alone and now without a job. Maybe God was testing her.

Autumn had been forced to try and find new roommates for their loft apartment, feeling lonely and more than a tad bitter. But the more she thought about two strangers moving into the place where she and her cousins had shared so much, the more she dreaded that happening. She didn't want new roommates.

Maybe coming home was the best option, even though she'd planned on working a few more years in New York before she wanted to consider moving back to Texas. But the city was big and gloomy without her cousins. And her father had always told her she had a place at Maxwell Financial Group any time she wanted to come home. He might even offer her a job here on the spot.

Richard marched her to the big den

toward the front of the Spanish-style house. "We can talk in private in here."

"Daddy, you're scaring me. Why all the secrecy?"

"Nothing secret, darlin'. Just wanted some quiet time with my little girl. I haven't had a minute with you over the last few days, and we've got a lot to talk about."

Autumn sank down on a chair, watching her father pace in front of the fireplace. "And I have a lot to tell you. Daddy, I—"

Richard held up a hand. "I'm just gonna come out and tell you, honey. I'm retiring from the firm."

"You are?" Surprised, Autumn held on to the arm of her chair. "When did you decide this?"

"Oh, right after your uncle Stuart died. I had been toying with the idea even before then, but his illness made me think. Our time here on earth is precious. And I want to spend more time with your mama and with the rest of my family, before it's too late."

"You're not sick?"

"No, no. I had me a little scare a while back, but the doctors tell me I'm as healthy as a horse these days. It's just that, well, it was time. The firm is in good shape. Very good shape."

Autumn let that information soak in, wondering what kind of scare her daddy had experienced. Surely her mother would have told her if anything bad had happened. "I'm glad to hear that you're okay, Daddy. And that the firm is solid. I'd love to—"

"Honey, I'd love to have you come back and work at the firm," Richard said, interrupting her yet again, as was his lovable way.

"Oh, Daddy." Autumn jumped up to hug him. "I was so worried. I didn't know how I was going to tell you—"

"Tell me what?"

"That I lost my job in New York. Downsizing." Seeing the shock on his face, she hurried to reassure him. "But I got a nice severance package and of course, I still have my stock, even though it's down because of this layoff. Anyway, I'm fine. But I don't want to stay in New York by myself."

Richard stood back, a grin splitting his face. "Well, San Antonio and El Paso, too. If that don't beat all. Good timing, huh? I'm sorry about your job, but I could sure use you at Maxwell. How 'bout you come to work for your ol' daddy again, honey?"

"I was hoping you'd say that," Autumn admitted, relief coursing through her. "I could find work in New York, but with everyone being back here—"

"You need to be back here, too," Richard finished, a soft smile on his face. "You know you always have a place here, Autumn."

"Yes, but I was just so afraid—"

Richard cleared his throat. "Listen, honey. When I decided back in the spring about retiring, well, I made some decisions I need to tell you about. There's just one little hitch to all of this—"

There he went, looking nervous again. He wasn't telling her the whole story, Autumn decided. The Maxwell men had a huge problem with communicating. She'd have to pry it out of him.

"Oh, and what would that be?" she asked, confused at his sheepish expression. Richard Maxwell never looked sheepish. And he never got nervous. Maybe he really was sick, and he was just afraid to tell her. "What's the hitch, Daddy?" she asked, repeating his words to her, her heart hoping he wouldn't give her bad news.

Then a tall figure cut through the sun rays streaming across the wide hallway.

"That would be me," Campbell said, his smile one-sided. "I'm the little hitch in this plan."

"What does he—"

Richard held Autumn by the arm, as if he expected her to bolt. "Uh, honey, that's what I needed to talk to you about. Campbell works for me. He took over the firm a few months ago, and just in time, too, I might add. And if you come back, well, you'd be working for—with—him now."

Autumn looked from her father to the

tall man standing with his hands in the pockets of his trousers, rocking back and forth on those ridiculous shoes. She turned back to Richard. "You mean, I won't be in charge of things?"

"Not just yet," Richard said, dread clear in his eyes. "It wouldn't be fair to Campbell. I've already given him the job."

Autumn waited while a sense of defeat settled over her system. "You hired a complete stranger to take over our family business, without even asking me how I'd feel about that?"

Richard nodded, then looked down at the woven rug. "Yep."

Autumn took in that one word, then nodded, trying to hide her disappointment. "Well, I guess that makes sense. I mean, I did say all along I wanted to keep working in New York."

"That's the impression I had, honey," Richard replied, clearly worried about her reaction. "I didn't want you to feel obligated to come back if you weren't ready."

Suddenly, all the signs were there. Her father had been acting strangely over the last few months. Cryptic and tight-lipped. April had urged Autumn to talk to him, but Autumn had been too busy at work to worry overmuch about her father back in Texas. She'd just chalked it up to grief over losing his older brother. Now, Autumn had to wonder if April had known about this and was afraid to tell her. April had probably insisted to Richard he be the one to break the news. And he should have been the one.

"Why didn't you at least mention this, Daddy?"

Richard shuffled and shrugged. "You just seemed so happy in New York, and you were making buckets of money. I didn't want you to feel pressured. I knew you had that infernal ten-year plan you've always talked about. I didn't want to mess with that, honey. I didn't want you back here out of some sense of misguided duty."

Autumn saw the sincerity in her father's eyes. "Well, that's awfully sweet of you, Daddy. But I'm afraid my ten-year plan has gone down the drain about halfway through."

"I hate to hear that," Richard said, "but hey, it all worked out for the best. You're here now, and you can work at Maxwell Financial Group, just like I've always wanted."

"You could have asked me about this sooner," Autumn said, seeing the doubt and concern in Campbell's eyes. "Whether I came back or not, I'm your daughter. I had a right to know. You didn't even ask me how I'd feel about this. You didn't even give me a chance to decide, either way."

"I'm asking now," Richard said. "Honey, I want you to be a part of the family business. I've always wanted that. You know that. And I have a plan myself—"

"Yeah, right," Autumn said, using her father's interrupting tactics to halt his next words. "*Me* working for *him*. That's your plan. I don't think that's going to work."

"Working *with* him," Richard corrected. "I've got it all worked out. I can set things up so you'll be an equal partner."

"Equal partner?" Autumn pointed a finger at Campbell. "I'm your flesh and blood, Daddy. I'd say that gives me a little more than equal benefits over some *interloper.* I won't have *him* bossing me around."

Campbell stepped farther into the room. "Hey, I'm a good boss." At her heated look, he quickly added, "Not that I'd ever boss you around. No, ma'am. I'm fun to work with and I'm fair. We'll do just fine together."

"Oh, I just reckon we would, but I'm afraid I'm not ready to have a partner," Autumn replied. Heading for the door, she said, "Thanks, but no thanks. I'll just take my chances somewhere else." She turned to leave the room, her eyes locking with Campbell's. "I can't take the job after all, Daddy. It would be rather awkward, coming back and having to deal with someone besides you at Maxwell Financial Group. I'm sorry we couldn't work this out, but…I'll find something else soon. I have lots of contacts all over the place. No need to worry about me."

She gave Campbell Dupree one last look, then she shot out the door and down the hall before she could do something really embarrassing, like bursting into frustrated tears.

Chapter Two

That had not gone very well.

Campbell pulled his sweet red classic '57 Corvette into the attached open garage of the cottage-style house he'd rented when he'd first arrived in Atlanta, Texas, his mind still reeling from the open hostility and hurt Autumn Maxwell had shown him at her cousin's wedding earlier today.

She didn't want to work with him. How was he going to put a spin on that with her father? Richard had gone on and on all summer about the possibility of Autumn one day coming back to the family business. He'd even put that stipulation in

Campbell's contract. And Campbell had agreed, thinking it would probably come a foot of snow in August before he'd ever have to worry about that happening.

He glanced around. "It's September," he reminded himself. "And the temperature is in the seventies."

Not a hint of snow among the tall pines, mushrooming oaks or aged hickory trees. The leaves on some of the trees were beginning to turn, but other than that, things looked perfectly clear.

Except the outlook on his future.

So what had happened today?

How had his life, the life he'd planned and mapped out the day he'd arrived here in this small town, suddenly become a confusing muddle?

Because of that lady with the pretty golden-brown eyes and beautiful auburn-streaked hair.

Autumn Maxwell. The boss's daughter.

How could such a pretty but aloof woman get to him in such a short time? Campbell prided himself on being able to read women. And on being able to charm them. His Cajun roots didn't allow for anything less.

Neither ability had worked on Autumn Maxwell. Now the burning question was, why? Or maybe, why not?

He'd thought about nothing else on the long ride back to Atlanta. The woman sure didn't want to be anywhere near the likes of him. Or maybe, she just didn't trust men, period. After all, she was a stuffy accountant type. Supposedly.

So are you, supposedly, he reminded himself. And maybe the woman was hostile because he'd taken over the company that would one day belong to her. Well, not so much taken over. Her father was still in charge. But Campbell was the wingman. So to speak.

He couldn't blame her. If someone else had swooped in and started running a company his family had owned forever, he'd probably be mad as a hornet, too. But then, Campbell thought with a twist of bitterness, his father had lost their family business long before Campbell had been old enough even to work there. That still didn't set well with Campbell, which was probably the reason he was now classified as a type A personality. A born workaholic, ruthless and too smart for his own good. That's how some described him.

But those same people sure didn't mind him investing their money and making them a killing in the stock market. Those people had probably never gone barefooted in the middle of winter or had to wear ratty, hand-me-down clothes from the second-hand store. They'd probably never had to beg for after-school jobs or work twelve-hour days in the soybean and sugarcane fields just to make ends meet.

Parking the car, Campbell turned off the engine and leaned back on the white leather headrest, closing his eyes to the fatigue that seemed to be pushing him down. The old days of stepping out of poverty, only to step on everyone else to get ahead, were long gone. He'd had to take a step back, reevaluate his tactics. He'd been fast approaching burnout down in New Orleans. It had only taken a couple

of panic attacks to show Campbell that he
needed to slow down, take things easy.
And it had only taken one quiet, rainy
evening sitting in an empty church somewhere in the Garden District to understand that God, not Campbell Dupree, was
the one in charge.

"So that's how you wound up here," he
reminded himself, his voice echoing
through the tiny garage. Campbell had
found God, and God had found Campbell
a place to hide out and find the rest he
needed so much.

But tonight, Campbell felt that old
restless energy swirling around him like
heat lightning. He couldn't wait to move
out to the beautiful cabin he'd found on
Caddo Lake. The cabin was being reno-
vated now, but soon Campbell would be
lost out there amid the moss-covered
cypress trees and the dark, blue-black
waters. The place reminded him of home,
of his grandfather's tiny cabin down near
Bayou Lafourche in southwest Louisiana.
Once his own more modern version of that
cabin was finished, he could fish all day

in his pirogue, or just float along with the current. Right now, he had to settle for weekend stays at the cabin.

Campbell Dupree, the risk taker, the adventurer, had a new set of rules: Work hard, but rest easy. Don't overdo working or playing. Stop. Look. Listen. Appreciate. Have faith.

At least these days, he had more time to devote to the simple life his long-dead grandfather had taught him to appreciate. No more burning the candle at both ends for the new and improved Campbell. No, sir. He might have given up all things Cajun and learned how to blend in with the mainstream world of business, but he could never turn his back on the values his *grand-père* Marlin Dupree had taught him.

"Stand still and consider the wondrous works of God."

That verse from Job came to Campbell now. His grandfather had always told Campbell that God was in charge, and that Campbell needed to relax and let God do his work.

But Campbell felt some of that old burning tension inside his gut, white-hot and fiery. Maybe his ulcer was coming back. Or maybe he was just worried about the pretty woman with the chestnut hair and amber eyes he'd left back in Paris. Autumn Maxwell.

He knew all about Autumn Maxwell. Her father doted on his only daughter. Richard had been so concerned about *not* bothering Autumn, however, he'd neglected to tell her that he'd suffered a light heart attack over a month ago. No one had that information, except Campbell and Autumn's mother, Gayle. It wouldn't do for a Maxwell man to look weak.

Especially not to the daughter who was too far away and too caught up in her work to be bothered. Somehow, though, Campbell got the impression that if Autumn had known about her father's health scare, she would have dropped everything to come back to Texas. She struck him as that kind of person. From everything her parents had told him, at least. And from the shining love he'd seen

in her eyes when she laughed and talked
with her family.

He envied that.

Campbell had been living underneath
Autumn's soft shadow since the first day
he'd set foot inside the plush but comfortable front-street offices of Maxwell Financial Group. Richard had made no
bones about how he wished Autumn
would come back and work for him. But
then he'd explained how Autumn lived in
New York and worked for some fancy
global accounting and finance firm.
Richard had hinted that he probably
couldn't begin to match her salary.
Campbell knew the particular firm mentioned and had to agree. Not too shabby.
Then Richard had shown Campbell a
picture of Autumn when she was younger.
Again, not too shabby.

"Why didn't I recognize her at first
today?" Campbell said as he shut the door
of the 'Vette and headed into the house.
He'd noticed her and realized who she
was only when she'd come walking up
the aisle of the chapel, her pretty dress

shimmering around her slender figure, her amber eyes bright with happy tears.

Well, she'd looked different today, stylish and all dolled up. The woman in the picture at the office had been younger, more fresh-faced and carefree in her jeans and flannel shirt, sitting on a horse. She'd been smiling.

The woman he'd offended today at the wedding had been sophisticated and polished, confident, but she hadn't smiled a whole lot.

"Okay, maybe she smiled a little bit," he said.

But not at him, Campbell reminded himself. She obviously was not impressed with the completely impressive Campbell Dupree.

If he really wanted to, Campbell thought as he poured himself a glass of milk, he could at least match her pedigree. He'd come from an old New Orleans family. Old money and a lineage that dated back to some broke but noble aristocrat in France—on his mother's side, at least. He knew his lineage was part English, part

French and sprinkled with Cajun from his father's side.

But he, just like his long-gone father, had disgraced his mother's family one time too many to use their geneology for leverage. No, Campbell Dupree did things his way. Always had and always would. And that included running Maxwell Financial Group. Only this time around, he'd have the guidance of God on his side, he prayed. This time around, Campbell would do things his way, but only after he'd prayed to God for help and understanding.

"Whether the heiress-apparent likes it or not."

Campbell downed his milk, clutched his aching stomach and wondered why it was so important that Autumn Maxwell *did* approve of him.

"So you don't approve of your father's choice to run the firm?"

Autumn turned to her mother, shaking her head. "I didn't say that. I just said he seems a bit too self- assured and arrogant for my taste."

Gayle Maxwell settled back in the over-stuffed chair in one of the many bedrooms of the Big M ranch house, one hand moving through her clipped auburn hair. "Funny, he reminds me so much of your father."

"Daddy?" Autumn's shocked expression reflected in the mirror of the antique vanity. Rubbing lotion over her freshly washed face, she laughed. "Mother, that man is nothing like my father."

"Not in looks," Gayle agreed, a hand touching the crocheted pillow she held in her lap. "But…the way he acts. Honestly, I think your daddy handpicked him because they are so much alike."

Autumn whirled to stare over at her mother, glad the family was staying here at the ranch for the weekend. She wasn't ready to go home to Atlanta and face Campbell Dupree just yet. "Why *did* Daddy pick him? I mean, why didn't he talk to me about all of this? I am his only child, after all."

Gayle shrugged, then carefully placed the lace pillow back behind her in the chair.

"We all urged him to do just that. But you know how stubborn your father can be. He refused to pull you away from your career in New York. He thought you were happy there."

"I was," Autumn admitted. "Then everything changed."

"Well, that's exactly what happened here, too," her mother said. "Your uncle Stuart passed on, then James decided to retire from gallivanting around and settle down in Athens. And—" She stopped, taking a breath.

"What?" Autumn asked, getting up to sit on the stool at her mother's feet. "What is it that y'all aren't telling me?"

"Your father had a light heart attack a few weeks back," Gayle said.

Autumn gasped. "Why didn't you call me?"

"He wouldn't let me," Gayle said. "He wouldn't even let me call James and Elsie. He didn't want to worry anyone. He said it was too soon after Stu's death." She took Autumn's hand. "He's fine now, honey, honestly. I watch him like a hawk and he's got a whole team of doctors lined up to help him. We are blessed that it was very mild." She shrugged. "You know how he is—he doesn't like to make a big deal out of things. I had to honor his wishes and keep this to myself." Then she looked down at the floor. "Of course, we had to tell Campbell—"

Autumn threw down her plastic lotion bottle. "Of course! Let's tell a perfect stranger, but not our own daughter. I don't get—" Then she stopped, her hand flying to her mouth at the distress on her mother's face. "I'm sorry, Mother. This isn't about Campbell and me. I know Daddy had his reasons, but it still doesn't sit very well. I'm just glad he's okay now."

Gayle nodded. "He is, honey. And he would have told you sooner, but, well, everything is changing so fast with our families these days. Death, weddings, retirements."

Autumn pulled a brush through her hair. "I guess so. I mean, Summer's grandparents moved into a retirement home without even letting her know a thing about it."

"Exactly," Gayle said, shaking her head. "It's almost too much to keep up with."

"And we were all three so caught up in our lives in New York. We should have communicated better."

"Not that it would have mattered," her mother replied. "Stubbornness and pride seem to be the dominating traits in our family tree."

Autumn got up to pace around the carpeted bedroom. "I don't understand the Maxwell men. Uncle Stuart kept his illness from April until it was almost too late for her to make it home in time to see him before he died. Uncle James had some sort of late-life crisis that had everyone thinking he was going to run off with some rodeo queen, until he broke down and told Summer and Aunt Elsie the truth—that he's just afraid of getting old. And now this with Daddy. Why can't they just open up to the people who love them?"

Gayle laughed again. "Because they *are* Maxwell men, honey. You know the stories and the legends. Rough and tumble, tough and ornery. Their ancestors helped win Texas from Mexico, helped build empires and conquer worlds, including everything from oil to railroads to the Alamo. They can't show any signs of failure or weakness. And they can't communicate for anything, I'm afraid."

Autumn had to agree there. "So he decided to retire after Uncle Stuart died?"

"No, actually just before he died. He hired Campbell back in the spring, but your father officially retired a few weeks ago."

"Right after the heart attack?"

"That pretty much sealed it, yes."

"But he decided way back?"

"Yes," Gayle said, puzzled.

"I knew it," Autumn said, bobbing her head. "I think April knew about this. I wonder why she didn't tell me?"

Gayle looked up at her. "Well, she's had a lot to deal with—her father's death, moving back to Texas from New York, starting a new job and planning a wedding. Don't blame her if she didn't put this at the top of her priority list."

"Oh, I'm not blaming April. She kept

urging me to call Daddy and talk to him. I blame myself—and him, of course."

"Like father, like daughter," her mother said, getting up to smooth the wrinkles out of her pink satin robe.

"I'm not quite as stubborn as Daddy," Autumn retorted.

"Oh, really? So you don't call it stubborn, turning your father down flat today?"

"That was before I knew about his heart attack. He just told me he'd had a little scare."

"More like a big scare for me," Gayle said. "I was so worried."

"But you didn't call me," Autumn said, her heart hurting with all the undercurrents running through this day.

"No, and I'm sorry for that," Gayle said. "But I promised your father I wouldn't tell anyone. And I'm sure he won't like it that I told you today. He'll think you feel sorry for him, and we wouldn't want that, now, would we?" She walked slowly to the door. "You know, honey, with you girls up there in New York, we just kind of let things slip by. No need to bother them—that's what we'd always say. I'm beginning to see that was wrong. We need our children around us, no matter good times or bad."

Autumn followed her mother to the door. "*He* needs me now, right?"

"Yes, he does. But he'd never admit that."

"You know I won't let him down, don't you, Mother?"

Gayle touched a hand to Autumn's face. "I know you will do the right thing, darling. You've always been a strong girl. And I know you love your daddy."

Autumn kissed her mother good-night, then turned to stare at herself in the mirror, the silence of the room echoing with a soft rhythm inside her brain. She could do this. She didn't have any other choice. She was out of work and at the end of the road. And her father needed her.

Autumn looked out the window at the starry night. "I hear You, Lord. I know when You close a window, You always open a door. Or is it when You close a door, You open a window?"

Either way, Autumn knew an opening when she saw one, and this one was clearly showing her the way home.

"I guess I'm going to work at Maxwell Financial Group," she told her worried expression as she turned back to the mirror. "And that means, I guess I'm going to work with Campbell Dupree. Whether I want to or not."

Autumn decided she'd need lots of extra prayers tonight. But then, so would Campbell Dupree.

Chapter Three

A motorcycle.

Autumn stared out the double windows of her father's office, watching as Campbell lifted his long legs off a big black-and-chrome motorcycle. He wore a business suit and a red helmet. And those irritating suede sneakers.

"Does he always arrive in such a showy manner?" April asked her father's secretary, Janice Duncan.

No one knew how old Janice was, and no one ever dared ask. She'd been a fixture at Maxwell Financial Group since Autumn was a baby. She'd had the same sensible short-clipped platinum hairstyle for as long as Autumn could remember. She never aged and she never, ever spoke about work or her personal life outside the office. Inside the office was another matter, however. She knew how to settle office squabbles and she knew how to peg new hires, and she didn't mind telling the Maxwell clan when she thought someone wouldn't make the cut. Autumn ranked Janice right up there with her own mother, trust-wise. So she knew she could depend on Janice to give her the goods, straight up, on Campbell Dupree.

"What's he driving today?" Janice asked, her green eyes never leaving the computer screen in front of her.

"Something Harley-Davidson, I think," Autumn said, careful to stand back so Campbell wouldn't look up and find her spying. "It's huge and shiny."

"Oh, that's nothing," Janice said, eyes smiling through her black-framed glasses. "He also owns a vintage Corvette and an overhauled Chevy pickup that he says used to belong to his grandfather back in

Louisiana." Then Janice grinned. "He's part Cajun, you know."

"No, I didn't know."

Autumn watched as Campbell greeted the president of the Chamber of Commerce as both men arrived for work, his whole body stance animated and sincere. Since the chamber was right across the street, it figured that Campbell would get to know the staff there. Friendly fellow, she thought. Waving to everyone in town, laughing and chatting it up on Main Street. Probably mostly for show.

"Is *he* from Louisiana?" she asked Janice, following the other woman into the next room so Janice could grab papers from the buzzing printer.

"That's what he told us. Grew up dirt-poor in some backwater bayou near the Gulf of Mexico."

"Hmm." Autumn gained a new respect for Campbell. He sure didn't look dirt-poor now. His suit was well-made and fitted him perfectly. The fancy monster bike he'd parked out front had to have cost a pretty penny. "I guess he's done okay for himself then."

"I'd say," Janice replied, her mind obviously on all the work she had to get done today. "He went to Tulane and Harvard, something about two different degrees. He's worked for some of the top firms in the South—one in that other Atlanta—you know, the one in Georgia that our town is named after."

"I've heard of the place, yes," Autumn said, grinning. "Where else?"

"Houston, Baton Rouge and New Orleans."

"Why does he move around so much?"

"Can't say," Janice said, stopping to stare at Autumn. "Why are you so curious?"

Autumn shrugged, then poured herself a cup of water from a nearby cooler. Her throat was dry this morning. "Well, I'd hate for him to run out on Daddy. What if he doesn't last? I mean, we're different here. Things move at a slow pace. I'm sure he's not used to that."

Janice gave her a wry smile. "Well, neither are you, city girl."

"Okay, I get it," Autumn said, smiling. "Enough questions, right? You have work to do and I'm hindering you."

"You used to do that on a regular basis, remember?" Janice said, her smile good-natured.

"I guess I did. After school, on Saturdays, during tax season."

Janice held up a hand. "Don't mention tax season, please. We don't have to worry about that until next spring." Then she gave Autumn a wide smile. "It is good to have you back, though. All grown up, but still Daddy's little girl."

Autumn heard the double doors of the reception area opening. "Well, Daddy's little girl is about to throw her weight around."

Janice lifted her eyebrows. "What? All one hundred pounds or so?"

"I weigh more than that," Autumn retorted, tossing her shoulder-length hair back off her neck. "But I hope I carry more weight around here than Campbell Dupree."

Janice grinned. "I do believe things are

about to change. Glad I didn't retire along with your daddy."

"I'll make it worth your time, I promise," Autumn told her as she pulled at her navy blazer. "Just watch."

"Oh, I intend to," Janice said to her departing back.

Campbell tossed his briefcase on one chair and his bag with two piping hot Danishes on the other, then stared at the woman standing by his desk. "Autumn? What a nice surprise. I think." He arched his neck, looking around toward the other office.

"My father's not here, if that's who you're looking for," Autumn said, her arms crossed, her eyes full of fire and dare.

Campbell braced himself, taking his own defensive stance while he took in her crisp tailored suit and even crisper white cotton blouse. Her shoes were a matching navy leather. Pumps. He'd always admired women who wore pumps.

Except this one had obviously come

dressed to kill. And he had the distinct feeling he was the one she was gunning for.

"So what can I do for you on this lovely fall day?" he asked, quickly moving his battered brown briefcase so she could sit down. If she wanted to.

She didn't. "Can the charm, Dupree. You and I have a few things to settle between us."

He watched the way her soft dark curls fell against the white collar of her prim blouse, giving her a look of pristine disarray. "Can I have my Danish and coffee first?"

Right on cue, Janice entered with a steaming mug, grinned at them, then left the room with raised eyebrows.

Autumn watched Janice beat a hasty exit. "Suit yourself." She didn't move a muscle, and her eyes never left his face.

"Look," he said, holding his hands out, palms up, "I know we didn't get off to a very good start the other day, but…you're here now. Let's start over."

She stood there like a pretty doll,

looking as if she might break if he touched her. So Campbell went about the business of lacing the coffee Janice had placed on his desk with two heavy creams. Then he set his strawberry cream cheese Danish out on a napkin, cut it down the middle, then sat down to stare up at her. "Want half?"

He breathed a sigh of relief when she sank down in one of the black-leather high-backed chairs across from his desk. She eyed the messy Danish with disdain. "No, thanks, I'm not hungry. And why didn't you take my father's office?"

That question threw him. "Because it's still your father's office. That won't change."

She pushed at the sensible silver clip holding her hair back off her face. "I can't believe he retired."

Campbell felt something deep in his heart turning as mushy as the inside of his Danish. "More like, you can't believe he retired and didn't tell you."

"That, too."

"That must have made you angry."

"More like, hurt."

"Well, don't be."

"Actually, I'm more hurt and concerned that he had a heart attack and told *you* instead of me."

"Only because I work for him."

"Right. But that's not the issue. The issue is his health and well-being."

"Yes, of course. And just to set your mind at ease, he's taking care of himself. Your mother is making sure of that."

"So she tells me."

"You don't look convinced."

"I'm kind of that way—I have to see something with my own eyes to believe it."

"I'll make a note of that."

She settled back against the chair, then crossed her long legs. Campbell caught a brief glimpse of her feet, and admired her shoes again. He almost missed the days of working with heavy-bellied, gray-haired, golf-playing executives back in New Orleans. Almost.

"I'm not going back to New York," she told him in an I-dare-you voice. "I'm going to stay right here and work. With you."

That sounded like a challenge, and he could never turn down a good challenge. So he stated the obvious. "With me."

"That's what I said."

"But you really don't want to do that, do you? I mean, work with me."

"No, not really. But then, we don't always get what we want, do we?"

"Amen to that."

They sat there staring across the mahogany desk at each other until Campbell once again offered her half of the Danish. He held it out, hoping she'd see it as a truce. Besides, he had another whole one for later in his bag.

Autumn took the flaky concoction, grabbing it and the napkin before the strawberry filling could fall out on her skirt. Then she eyed his coffee.

"Want some?"

"I could use a good strong cup. But I like mine black."

He got up. "I'll file that away for future reference."

"Where are you going?"

"To make you a pot of strong black coffee."

He thought he saw admiration flickering in her eyes. And he couldn't help the smile that split his face as he headed down the hall to the break room.

Two hours later, they had talked about everything from 401(k) accounts, penny stocks and mutual funds to overhauling Social Security. They'd covered real estate investments, capital gains, market losses, asset management and property and estate taxes.

They'd just polished off the second Danish—this one apple—and a whole pot of coffee.

Campbell sat back in his chair, his hands clasped at the back of his neck. "Okay, you win. I haven't been able to trip you up on anything financial."

"Were you trying to trip me up?" Autumn asked, comfortable with him for the moment. She'd sure had fun discussing work with him. Too much fun.

"Weren't *you* trying to trip me up?" he retorted, his winning smile almost winning her over.

Almost. But not quite yet.

"I just wanted to make sure you—"

"You wanted to make sure I wouldn't run your father's company into the ground," Campbell finished for her, his eyes glistening like diamond chips. "I can appreciate that."

"Wouldn't want it any other way, right?" Autumn countered, enjoying the back and forth of their conversations. That should irritate her, but it didn't. Not a good sign. That and the fact that Campbell Dupree was right on target with his financial savvy and his math skills. She couldn't find anything else to nitpick about.

"That's right." He leaned forward in his chair, his hands dropping over the stacks of clutter on his desk. The man obviously didn't believe in organization. "I wouldn't have taken this job if my only purpose was to do in Maxwell Financial Group, Autumn. That wouldn't do me any good, now, would it?"

She caught the hint of Cajun in his words. It was in the inflection, in the way his eyes gleamed, in the way he tilted his head to one side. Lethal. If this man really wanted to turn on the charm, she knew it would be killer.

Why was he showing so much restraint around her? Well, she was the boss's daughter. And he was minding his p's and q's, no doubt.

"No, I guess you want to make money right along with the rest of us," she said in answer to his question. "And you seem to be very good at your job."

"I try."

"Will my being here bother you?"

He gave her a look that made her think he was already bothered with her being here. And then he confirmed that notion. "Most definitely."

"But you will behave and help me adjust, right?"

"For sure."

"And we both agree that my father is still in charge, even if he spends more time on the golf course now than in the office?"

"He's the boss."

"And we both agree that we only want the best for our clients and their investments, right?"

His eyes flirted while she spoke. "Absolutely."

"And we can be equal partners. No special privileges just because Richard Maxwell is my father. We're a team."

"We are most definitely a team. I'm here to work for your father and our clients. I expect you to do the same."

"Good, then. I think I can work with you." She prayed. She hoped. She'd have to be careful with that throwing-her-weight-around stuff.

"I know I can work with you."

His confidence was inspiring.

He stood up, reached out a hand. She took it and shook hands with him, very much aware of the warmth of his touch, of the firm, confident way he shook her hand. Very much aware of the way his eyes locked with hers in that bold, daring look. Campbell was willing to take her on, but she figured he was also willing to toy with her just a bit. Just to keep things interesting.

"I'm glad we talked this out," he finally said, letting go of her hand.

Autumn felt warm and cold at the same time. Maybe this was a bad idea, after all. Just thinking about being here, day in and day out, with this man around, caused her to break out in hives.

"Work," she said, clearing her throat. "We have to focus on the work, Campbell. Not our own agendas."

"Yes, ma'am."

"Are you listening?"

"Yes, ma'am."

Autumn got up, then stood with her hands on the back of her chair. "Okay, you have to stop that."

He shrugged, shuffled some papers. "Stop what?"

She touched a hand to her collar, moved her head around. "That…that thing you do with your eyes."

"It's called looking."

"Well, you can't look at me that way."

"What way is that?"

"You know what way. I'm not one of your conquests, Campbell...I'm...We have to be serious, focused, determined."

"I am all of those things, I can assure you. And how do you know about my conquests?"

"Just a calculated guess."

"Hmm."

She came around the chair and leaned across the desk, her knuckles turning white as she balanced her hands on the cool glass-covered surface. "Okay, here's the deal. I am going to stay here in Atlanta for a few months and work here at Maxwell. Only because my father needs me to do so, and only because I lost my job in New York and it's lonely there without April and Summer. And only until I can decide what to do next. You are going to respect me, and confer with me, and treat me as an equal partner in all matters concerning this business. I go by the book and I follow the rules. I hope that's clear."

"Crystal."

"And while we're discussing this—I don't bring personal business to work, I work hard and I work late. And if you buy breakfast, you might need to know I like my coffee black and I like half a bagel with a little fruit on the side. I don't date coworkers and I don't like flirting in the workplace. Is that clear?"

He got up, leaned his hands on the desk and brought his head down until they were face-to-face, nose to nose and eye to eye. "Very clear. Now let me tell you a few things about me and how I operate. I know how to make money for people. It's a gift that I will never take for granted. I admire and respect your father, so you can rest easy that I will always put this company's best interests first. I like to come in early and work late, but I also sometimes like to take long rides on my Harley, just to clear my head."

"I assume you pay exorbitant insurance rates on that thing?"

"That and my Corvette, but I've got the funds to cover it and I enjoy my toys."

"Suit yourself. What else do you want to tell me?"

He thought about it for a minute, as if there was so much more he had to say. "I like new experiences, and I like getting to know other people. I like my coffee heavy with cream, and I have a sweet tooth the size of this state. I don't eat liver, but I do like gumbo made with duck or turkey, even though seafood gumbo is my favorite."

She grinned. "Well, who doesn't like gumbo? Go on."

Campbell grinned right back. "So this is Campbell Dupree 101?"

"I'm learning a lot. Keep spilling it, Dupree."

"You might not like what you hear."

"I told you, I like to know things. I need proof."

He gazed over at her, that challenge in his eyes again. "Okay, I have a weakness for King Cake and pralines, but I work off things like that by getting out and living a little, staying active. So don't panic if I don't jump when you say jump, or if it seems as if I'm not working when I really am." He tapped a finger to his forehead. "I don't always go by the book, but it's always on, inside my brain."

"Is that it?"

He nodded, still too close. "Oh, there is one other thing."

She breathed in the scent of something fresh and clean. His shampoo or soap, and maybe a little strawberry. "What?"

His eyes moved over her face, touching on her lips. "I like to flirt. A lot. But I don't intend to do that with you, because I am also a professional, and because I respect you way too much to make you feel uncomfortable. However, sometimes, I slip up and break all the rules. I just want to be clear on that, okay? So cut me some slack."

Autumn stood straight up, casting her eyes down just so she could catch her breath. "I don't like cutting people any slack," she said, sending him a confident look in spite of the shaking of her hands. "I'll just have to ignore that side of you—a lot."

Then she turned and hurried out of his office, her back straight, her heels clicking a hasty path away from him and his rules he aimed to break.

He was just that kind of man—the kind
who could cause a woman to break all
the rules right along with him.

She needed another drink of water.

Chapter Four

"So how are things at work, honey?"

Autumn looked up from the papers she'd been going over to find her mother staring down at her. From the look of concern marring her mother's oval face, Autumn figured Gayle was more worried than curious. Why did everyone around here seem to be walking on eggshells? Did they all think she'd have some sort of breakdown, throw a hissy fit if things didn't go her way?

Autumn had always prided herself on being the calm one. She had watched on more than one occasion as April told people off in classic, understated tones, and she'd watched, cringing, as Summer went at people with gusto, never holding back. Autumn held back, analyzed the situation, thought things through, then determined how best to handle the situation. She didn't throw fits.

Or at least she hadn't until she'd come home to find a squatter taking over the family business. Now it seemed as if everyone in Cass County was giving her a wide berth. Which meant she had to be extremely diligent in her professionalism and her loyalty to her father's legacy. She couldn't taint the Maxwell name, after all. Especially over some handsome, irritating, smart-aleck intruder like Campbell Dupree.

An intruder who kept a worn Bible amid the clutter on his desk, she reminded herself. Don't think about the nice parts, she also reminded herself. Don't think of him as anything but a coworker. And most of the coworkers she'd known were ruthless and cutthroat, out to get ahead no matter who got in their way. Campbell would probably do the same, regardless of whether that meant stepping all over the boss's daughter.

She looked at her loving, serene mother, and told herself not to allow any of her own bitterness and misgivings to cloud her mother's beautiful face.

"We've been busy," Autumn said, careful to choose just the right words. Her mother could always tell whenever Autumn was hedging. "The firm is solid, Mama. Our clients are happy and we've reassured most of them to ride out these latest market fluctuations. We're planning a financial seminar in a couple of weeks, just to acquaint our clients with Campbell and me. That should bring in some new clients, too—"

Gayle held up a hand, her diamond-encrusted bracelet watch slipping down her arm. "I don't need to know the financial status of the firm, Autumn. Your daddy brags about that with every waking breath. The man lives and breathes IRAs, SEPs and mutual funds. He's very proud, you know. I was asking more about how things are going between you and Campbell."

"Oh, that." Autumn shrugged, then twirled her gold pen between her fingers just long enough to put on a blank face. "Honestly, we stay so busy, I can't really comment, other than to say he is good at what he does."

Very good, she wanted to add. Very good at being charming, very good at being up-to-date, no matter how hard she tried to stay ahead of him, very good at making strong coffee and crunching numbers to the point that she wanted to weep from the sheer beauty of the man's brain, and very good at smiling up at her each time she walked into his office.

In fact, the man smiled at her even when she was frowning at him. Which was just about every time she ran into him. She'd enter frowning, and somehow, he'd have her exiting with a laugh. It just wasn't fair. Accountants were supposed to be stoic and studious, weren't they? Accountants weren't supposed to ride in red shiny things or big loud machines, were they? And surely, accountants weren't supposed to look as laid-back and unconcerned as a rodeo clown, were they? The man wore sneakers to work. He talked about all these grand, daring adventures he'd been on, around the world and back. Hiking, biking, mountain climbing, fishing, sailing. You name it, Campbell had done it. She hoped the man had a good life insurance policy.

"So you two have hit it off?" Gayle asked, looking over her reading glasses at Autumn.

"We work well together," Autumn responded.

He was spontaneous and disorganized.

She was anal-retentive and compulsively organized.

Yeah, they worked well together, all right.

"Are you sure?" Gayle asked as she settled across the breakfast table from Autumn, a copy of the *Citizens' Journal* rustling in her hands. "I mean, are you two really getting along? Your father is in such a tizzy, worrying about this."

"Tell Daddy not to worry," Autumn said, dropping her pen and looking over at her mother. "I don't want him worried about anything. Campbell and I are working together and we both agree that we won't bring personal agendas into the work-place."

Gayle let out a gentle gasp, her eyes going wide. "But you do have…personal agendas?"

Autumn felt the flush of entrapment moving down her face. Beneath that deb-utante demeanor, her mother was shrewd and all-knowing. She needed to remember that. "No, that's not what I meant. I'm just saying that we know how to be profes-sional. We're working toward the common goal, to keep Maxwell running smoothly. And Daddy is welcome to check in on us any time he wants."

"Oh, I know that," her mother said, smiling. "In fact, he's on his way to the office right now, to have a nice long break-fast meeting with Campbell."

Autumn jumped up, shuffling papers. "He is? Then I'd better get over there. He might have questions for me."

Gayle's carefully arched brown brows

rose as she stared up at Autumn. "No need to hurry, honey. Your father specifically wanted some private time with Campbell. You know—the old-boy network."

Autumn could feel her hackles rising. Telling herself to calm down, she stopped stuffing papers in her Burberry briefcase. "Oh, really. And just what does Campbell Dupree have to say that I can't hear? Is he already undermining me to my own father?"

"I didn't say that now—"

"But you said this is a private meeting. I thought I was supposed to be an equal partner. And already they're having closed-door meetings behind my back?"

She was halfway to the back door when she heard her mother's low chuckle. Turning, Autumn perched a hand on her hip. "And just what is so funny, Mama?"

Gayle held a fist to her mouth. "Oh, my. You, suga'. The way you tossed all those papers in your briefcase, the way you were heading out the door, all bent on doing battle—I'd say there is a whole lot of something personal going on between you and Campbell. A healthy competition, at least."

"Competition is good," Autumn said, taking a deep breath and wishing she'd kept her cool about this. Obviously, her mother had been waiting for just such a show of insecurity and pettiness. "And competition is nothing personal. It's all about business—my father's business."

"How could any of us forget that?" Gayle asked, still smiling. "You would walk through fire for your daddy, I do believe."

"Yes, I would," Autumn said, thinking that the last couple of weeks working with Campbell had been like walking through fire. At times, she felt hot and clammy, other times cold and alone. She just never knew what to expect with Campbell. And she prided herself on always knowing what to expect, had trained herself to stay ahead of the competition and the circumstances.

Her cousins prayed and planned. Autumn prayed and calculated. That was just how her brain worked. She'd need lots of prayers and lots of calculations to stay one step ahead of Campbell. After all, they had been put in charge of safeguarding the incomes of their clients. It wouldn't do for them to have infighting, like the money changers of old. Not that she thought Campbell was corrupt. The man seemed as stable and honest as the midsummer days were long. But in spite of her trust and awe of him, Autumn was watching and praying. She hoped her own values and God's good graces would help her in dealing with her new partner.

I won't let him wear me down, she told herself as she tried to regain her composure. Then she turned to her overly curious, overly grinning mother. "I think I have time for one more cup of coffee, Mama. Tell me what you have planned for today. Oh, and tell me all about that new perfume you bought the other day. I might have to try some of that. You know I love good-smelling body lotion."

Gayle smiled, made a big, long-drawn-out deal of pouring more coffee and buttering more raisin toast. "How lovely that we get to spend some time together this morning."

"Isn't it, though," Autumn replied, her foot tapping on the tile floor underneath the long breakfast table. "We should do this more often."

"Yes, we should," her mother said, her eyes gleaming. "I have an early meeting at church this morning, but we have a little while before we both head out. Did I tell you I'm working on the stewardship committee? We're planning a big celebration to show our thanks for having a solid financial plan and wonderful tithing members."

"This family thrives on working with money," Autumn said. "Even in church, apparently."

Gayle grinned. "Money can be the root of all evil, but if used wisely, it can also make a difference in this old world. We're able to help so many people with our mission work and with our food bank and soup kitchen. But it does take a lot of money to finance those things."

"I guess it's in the blood," Autumn

replied. "But I'm thankful that we're so blessed. Which is why I have to be protective of Maxwell Financial Group."

"I wouldn't want it any other way," her mother replied.

"Neither would I." Autumn tried to chew her toast, all the while wondering what her father and Campbell could possibly be discussing.

They were discussing her.

Campbell sat up straight, feeling as if he'd been called into the principal's office just as he had many, many times during his school years.

"So, you and my little girl getting along okay?" Richard asked again, his eyes full of enough steel and daring to hold back a gusher.

"Yes, we certainly are," Campbell repeated, feeling hot under the collar of his starched shirt. "At least, I think we are. Has Autumn said otherwise?"

"No," Richard replied, tapping his fingers on his desk. "Why would she, if there's not a problem?"

"No problem," Campbell said, deciding this was a test of some sort. A test that felt like walking through a minefield. He leaned back in his chair, prepared to defend his honor and his reputation if necessary.

But when he thought back over the last week, he knew both his honor and his reputation had been sorely tested at every turn. Tested by the scent of some sort of floral perfume that reminded him of midnight in a New Orleans courtyard. Tested by the click of high heels against tile floor and the slamming of a door just across the hall. Tested by amber-hued doe eyes and auburn curls that begged to be touched. Tested every which way by a woman who remained very serious and businesslike, no matter how much he tried to charm her. Autumn's work habits were precise and unencumbered. She arrived at nine o'clock on the dot and stayed well past five. She cloistered herself in her office, buried herself in data and print-outs, then called clients, using her Southern manners, to win them over and reassure them. Then she'd triumphantly march over to his office, her expression all business, and announce they'd snagged yet another high-dollar client. All in a day's work. And all the while, Campbell couldn't concentrate on his own clients and files.

He was slowly losing his grip.

"The books look good," Richard said now, rocking back in his leather swivel chair. "Clients are happy. Well, most of them, anyway."

"You've been over the files?" Campbell asked, glad to be on a subject he could handle.

"Of course. I've checked all the data and I've kept up with the markets. I've made sure our clients with conservative long-term investments feel comfortable having a new man on board. I'm here to reassure our clients. You know people get itchy when their money is being bandied about. But we're fine, just fine. New management does not mean anybody around here is going to lose any money. Things are in order, as is to be expected. But then, I never for one second doubted that."

Regaining his equilibrium, Campbell sat up. "Okay, then, why don't you explain what you are doubting? Because it's obvious you called me in here today for a reason. And I'm beginning to think that reason has nothing to do with our accounts."

"You are correct," Richard said, deadpan. "I'm just concerned about my little girl, is all."

Campbell let out a breath. "Well, in case you haven't noticed, she's not a little girl anymore. She's a woman, a smart, self-assured, calculating, infuriating, completely grown-up woman who's really quite smart. Remarkable."

Richard let out a whoop that caused the rafters to shake. "So…she's getting to you, right?"

Campbell dropped his head, then nodded. "With every waking breath. Your daughter is one tough taskmaster."

"I taught her that, you know," Richard said through a triumphant grin. "You can't get a thing past Autumn."

"Tell *me,*" Campbell replied, glad to

admit the truth at last. "But then, I hope you understand, I don't want to slip anything past Autumn, or you, for that matter. I like my job, and I enjoy my work here. I like living here. And I'd like to stay alive—so don't think you have to get the shotgun after me."

"Thought never entered my mind," Richard said, his grin saying exactly the opposite.

Campbell swallowed. "I really do want to live to see my old age, Richard."

Richard waved a hand in the air. "So you think you made the right decision, giving up all that fancy-schmancy big-city stuff for a small-town accounting firm?"

Campbell nodded. "I know I made the right decision. I'm more rested, a lot more healthy and I'm learning to enjoy life. I'm sure not as stressed and overworked as I was back in New Orleans. So if you were worried that your daughter coming home might be a distraction, well, I have to level with you—it has been. She has been. But, I can handle that. Autumn and I are both professionals."

"I never doubted that either, son."

Campbell felt a sudden warmth flooding through his system at the word *son*. He'd been forced to grow up without a father, and he'd often wondered what it would be like to have a whole, loving family surrounding him. His grandfather Marlin had always taught him that the real Father would always guide Campbell, if he'd just let Christ into his heart. It had taken him a long time and a near-miss health crisis to realize that.

"But you must have been doubting me," Campbell replied to Richard's reassurance. "Just a little bit?" At Richard's confused look, he added, "You are a very protective father, Richard. I admire that and I'll probably be the same way if I ever have a daughter. But you have my word—Autumn and I understand each other. Strictly business. It's all about Maxwell Financial Group."

Richard got up, held out his hand. "Good. That's good. 'Cause I'd hate to have to hurt you, son. Just remember that.

If you hurt Autumn, I'll have to hurt you. It wouldn't be pretty."

"I understand," Campbell said, his heart racing, his smile feeling like plastic on his own skin. "I don't need that kind of grief. Boss's daughter, that kind of thing. No, sir. Not gonna happen."

He was still smiling as he waved Richard out the door. "Have a good golf game at the club today, sir."

When he was sure that Richard Maxwell had indeed left the premises, Campbell let out another sigh and leaned his forehead against the door of his office. Then he felt a hand on his arm.

He looked up. "Janice?"

"Here," the secretary said, sympathy in her eyes. "Take these."

"What is it?" Campbell asked, grateful for the cup of water she offered, but apprehensive about the pills in her hand.

"Vitamins." Janice smiled sweetly. "You'll need them, trust me."

"You heard all of that?"

"Campbell, I've worked here a long time. I've heard that speech years back with every boy who ever even thought about looking twice at Autumn Maxwell."

"He'd kill me if I did anything to hurt her, wouldn't he?"

Janice nodded. "Even though he truly is a forgiving, God-fearing man, I'm quite sure of it. But, you are a seasoned professional. No need to worry on that regard. I think you can live a nice long life as long as you toe that line."

Campbell nodded, swallowed the big vitamins and his water, then headed into his office. "I am in serious trouble here," he whispered, wondering whether he should pray or pack his bags.

He knew in his gut that each day he worked beside the intriguing, stubborn, wonderfully prim Autumn Maxwell was yet another day he only wanted to grab her and whisk her away to get to know her better: to kiss her, to laugh with her, to make her laugh at him, to unravel that tightly held facade she had so carefully woven around herself. But he'd just promised her father that he didn't have any such intentions.

"I need help, Lord," Campbell said. "I really need to focus on my work, not my work partner."

And then he lifted his nose and inhaled the scent of jasmine and gardenia, the scent that reminded him of home and family and a soft, cool wind blowing through an open window, a scent of longing and sweetness. And he knew she was in the next room. Campbell looked at the clutter on his desk, clutched at the sharpening pain in his gut, and decided he needed to put his nose to the grindstone. He'd come too far to turn back now. He'd gone through fire and he'd come out on the other side with a new perspective on life and work. He couldn't, wouldn't turn away from the plow.

Even if this whole office did suddenly smell like a garden of delight.

Chapter Five

"So tell me what you and my father talked about the other day." Autumn turned from pouring herself a glass of water and waited for Campbell to respond to her question.

It was well past sunset on a Wednesday night. They'd worked all day preparing for the free financial seminar they were offering at a nearby hotel at the end of the week. They'd been so focused, Autumn hadn't had a minute to ask Campbell about his early-morning meeting the day before with her father.

She waited, sipping her water, as Campbell took his dear sweet time in answering her. While she waited, she watched him at work. The man really was fascinating. He read over the final drafts of their agenda for tomorrow night, his brow furrowed, his hair ruffled. He'd long ago loosened his silk tie—the cute one with the wood ducks marching across it in a perfectly symmetrical design—and rolled up his shirtsleeves. He just about always wore crisp white shirts to work, but today he'd chosen a light baby blue that made his eyes turn from a sparkling velvet brown to an almost night black. Every now and then, he'd rake a tanned hand across that little flip of bangs hanging down on his forehead. Then he'd go right back to furrowing his brow, his focus complete and undisturbed.

"Hey, you," Autumn said, fatigue weighing her down as she stood near the microwave in the combination break-room/extra work space in the back of the offices. "I asked you a question."

"I heard you," he said, finally raising his head, one vertebra at a time. He lifted a finger. "Just hold that thought."

Autumn didn't like having to hold her

thoughts. "I'm going to check my e-mail before we call it a night," she replied, doubtful that he'd even heard her. She couldn't fault him for being thorough. This seminar was important to both of them, not only for reassuring their existing clients, but also for bringing in new ones from the surrounding towns. They'd give their professional pitch, make viable financial suggestions, then take questions. It should bring in some new blood and make them even busier than they were now. Autumn liked being busy.

It kept her out of trouble.

Sitting down at her desk, Autumn logged on to see if her cousins April and Summer had responded to her oh-so-carefully worded report of her first week at Maxwell Financial Group. She'd glossed over the little charges of electricity that seemed to hiss and spark every time she was near Campbell. She just hoped her two cousins had bought it.

Apparently, they had not.

The first reply was from April, and she'd copied Summer on it.

Autumn, sounds as if you're fitting right in back in your daddy's business. I never had any doubts. But before I get into the juicy details of what's brewing between you and the interesting Campbell Dupree, I just wanted to tell both of you that Reed and I are blissfully, sweetly happy. Our honeymoon in Santa Fe was so wonderful. I got to see some of the places where my mother had traveled and we visited the gallery there where some of her paintings are hanging right beside the Georgia O'Keeffes. We also caught up with long-lost family members on my mother's side. Mother would have been so proud and touched. Reed was so sweet and understanding. What can I say? I love that man.

Things at the Big M are kicking right along. We've got guests booked well into next spring and everyone here is excited and thrilled to be a part of this new venture. I've hired very capable managers so I can continue my PR work at Satire on a part-time basis and make my rounds to the department stores, and Reed is here to watch over everything. Life is good. Now, enough about me.

Summer, we need a full report on how things are going for you and Mack and sweet little Michael. Let us know soon! And let us know when you two finally set a date for your wedding. I can't wait to help find you the perfect gown. Now, back to you, Autumn.

Just what really is going on at Maxwell Financial Group? I get the feeling that you've finally met your match in Campbell Dupree, but you seem to have left out so many important details. Of course that just means you're avoiding the real issues. Tell us everything, and I do mean everything. You deliberately left out all the good information about Mr. Dupree. Is he single? Does he have a dark past? Is he trustworthy in taking over things for Uncle Richard? We want to know the details.

"Busted," Autumn whispered through a defeated sigh. She had to wonder if the whole state of Texas could feel the attraction between Campbell and her. She scanned the other business related e-mails, then saw one from Summer.

"Okay, here comes the other one," she said, smiling.

Summer didn't waste any time.

Really, April, you shouldn't go on and on about your exceedingly boring and happy life. Some of us have issues to deal with in our own love lives. (Grin). Seriously, I am so glad that you have found some peace. As for me—Mack and I are taking things very slowly and one day at a time. We have to tread lightly so that Michael can adjust to losing his mother and accepting the father he never knew he had. Then you add me into the equation—well, you get the picture. But I love both of them, and MeMaw assures me that with lots of prayer and faith, we will all be okay. Michael loves my grandparents and they have fallen for him, too. So we're all cautiously optimistic here. Not sure when we'll get married, but we will one day. So just hold your horses and keep dieting so you both can fit into your bridesmaids' dresses.

Now, Autumn, spill your guts, girl. Did you think we wouldn't notice how you conveniently left out the interesting tidbits of your sparring with Campbell Dupree? You always get quiet about a subject when that very subject is on your mind. So tell us what's really up at Maxwell Financial Group, and I mean besides supermarket stock and long-term estate planning.

"Double busted," Autumn said, rotating her head to relax her knotted neck muscles.

She'd just begun to type in a reply to both her cousins when she felt two warm, strong hands on her neck.

Glancing back, she saw Campbell standing over her at about the same time as she felt the gentle pressure of his hands massaging her neck. She let out a little gasp, then quickly closed her e-mail folder.

"I...I didn't hear you...oh, that feels wonderful."

"I'm good at neck massages," he said, the intimacy of his words echoing out over the quiet office. "But I don't want to overstep the boundaries, so tell me to stop and I will."

"No, no," she said, feeling naughty, but oh, so much more relaxed. "You...you have a gentle touch. I didn't realize how...tense I was."

"We worked hard today," he said, his hands pressing against the bunched muscles just above the ballerina neckline of her green cashmere sweater. "How about we get a bite to eat before we go our separate ways?"

Autumn pushed up out of her chair and immediately missed the warmth of his touch. "Uh, is that such a good idea? I mean, it's late and..."

He leaned back on the credenza beside her desk, then crossed his arms over his chest. "And that, too, would be overstepping?"

She shrugged. "I'm not sure. Would this be coworkers sharing a meal, or a man and a woman out on a date?"

His smile was just as endearing as his disheveled hair. "Well, I have noticed that you are definitely a woman and I am a man, but we do work together, so technically, it would be coworkers taking a break—together." Then he held up his hands as if in surrender. "No strings attached. Strictly the last wish of a starving man before he crashes for the night."

Warnings bumped and jumped throughout Autumn's system like a ticker tape jamming a machine. "I could go for a burger," she finally said. "Nothing fancy."

He pushed off the credenza. "Nothing fancy. And I think I know just the place."

Autumn turned off her computer. She'd e-mail her cousins a full and glowing report once she got home. Right now, she just wanted to relax and get her thoughts in order before their big day tomorrow.

And she really wanted to pin Campbell down about that meeting he'd had with her father.

"Tell me about this truck," she said to Campbell a few minutes later. He'd insisted they ride together to the greasy spoon restaurant out near Caddo Lake. To talk business, of course.

Campbell grinned, then shifted the groaning gears attached to the column on the steering wheel. The old Chevy bounced along. Not exactly a comfortable ride, but very clean and updated.

"My grandfather Marlin Dupree bought this truck in the late fifties. He never replaced it. He was a young man when he bought it and he was well over ninety when he died last year. So—"

Autumn held on for dear life and laughed. "So you're telling me this truck is almost fifty years old?"

"That's right. Can't you tell?"

"Not really. I mean, it's obvious it's vintage. But it's so pretty. You must have completely overhauled it."

"I did," he said, nodding as he turned the steering wheel. "No power steering," he said through a groan. "He kept it in pristine condition, so it was just a matter of having the seats recovered—"

"In this pretty cream and blue," she interrupted, running a hand over the soft leather.

He grinned again, shot her a quick look. "Yes, that and having some detail work done on the interior and rebuilding the engine. It's a perfect replica of a real '57 Chevy. It *is* a real '57 Chevy."

"You like getting involved in the details, don't you?" she asked, impressed that he'd so lovingly overhauled his grandfather's truck. "But then, I guess you loved your grandfather, right?"

"With all my heart."

He grew silent then, as if he'd traveled somewhere far away in his mind. Autumn thought about April's question in her e-mail. *Does he have a dark past?*

"Do you miss him?" she asked, then she lifted a hand in the air to halt his answer. "Dumb question. Of course you miss him."

"I do," he replied, his eyes on the road. "He was a very important part of my life."

He pulled the truck into the parking lot of the Busy Burger, then turned to her. "Here's my story—I was born near Bayou Lafourche, Louisiana, to a poor Cajun man named Timothy Dupree and a social-ite mother named Margaret Gerard. They had to get married because of me. My mother's wealthy family disowned her. I was never really close to them, but now both my maternal grandparents are dead and gone and dat's dat, as the Cajun like to say. My father left when I was around five and my mother never quite got over that. So she went to work every day as a secretary at a large oil corporation and ne-glected me, a lot, because she had bills to pay and a son to provide for. She took care of all the basic needs, but she kind of went numb on me in the maternal, emotional-needs department. My *grand-père* Dupree and a whole slew of aunts and uncles and cousins raised me, which suited my mother just fine.

"I still keep in touch with all of them.

And I still visit my mother on the required holidays of Easter, Thanksgiving and Christmas.

"She divorced my absent father when I was a teen and married her boss at the oil company. He was a man more in keeping with what her folks thought appropriate as far as marriage and a future were concerned. He keeps her in high style down in New Orleans. We're not very close. But I've forgiven her. I've forgiven all of them. And I have my grandfather to thank for that. He gave me that little kernel of faith to carry with me everywhere. At times, I was too blinded and too dumb to see that God had a hand in all my choices. But my *grand-père* knew. He always knew. And he had a whole legion of people—my angels, he used to say—watching after me. That is why I honor him still. That is why I love this truck." He sighed, his hands falling loosely across the steering wheel. "Now can we please eat?"

Autumn sat in shock, her heart bursting with the pain he must have felt at being tossed about by his parents. How could a family do that—just disinherit someone because they didn't approve of a child's existence? She couldn't imagine that happening in her family. The Maxwells had all welcomed little Michael, Mack's young son, with open arms. And no judgment. But then, they had the same strong faith system that Campbell's grandfather obviously had possessed.

Thank You, God, for that, she said in a silent prayer.

"I'm sorry," she finally said, wondering if she'd made him angry by asking questions. "I didn't mean to pry."

"You're curious," he replied, opening his squeaky door. "It's natural. I just like to get the necessary things out in the open right away. So there you have it. My life in a nutshell."

"Oh, I think there's more," Autumn said as she hopped down out of the truck. "But I'm not so sure you're willing to open up completely to me."

He met her as she came around the tailgate. "Do you want to know more? Are you willing to hear all about me? Or are you just being kind?"

She hesitated, thinking she was dying to know everything, for some odd reason. "You were right. It's just curiosity." To lighten things, she added, "And you should know by now, I am never kind."

He reached for her then, his hand grasping her arm to hold her there, his eyes searching her face with an expression full of remorse and longing. "I know you can be kind," he said, his voice husky and close. "I want you to *want* to be kind to me, but I don't want any sympathy. I have a good life now. I'm safe. I'm okay."

Safe. That a man who seemed as carefree and adventurous as Campbell would simply want to be safe—that surprised her. And only made him more endearing and interesting to her.

"I can see that, Campbell," she said, his nearness causing little shock waves to bristle down her spine. "And I'll tell you this—I'm not offering pity or sympathy. I'm trying to tell you how much I admire you. You've obviously overcome whatever obstacles you had in your childhood. My practical side does admire that. But my, uh, *kind* side wonders if you're still trying to overcome the pain you must feel at times."

He stepped back, stared down at her. "Don't try to figure me out, Autumn. I'm just a man who was lost once. Now I've found my way. I only ask that you don't push me away, because I need to be here, right here, working for your father, now."

Did Campbell think she was fishing for information just so she could report back to her father and push him out of the business? Did he really think she was that ruthless?

"I wasn't planning on shoving you out the door," she said, a little spark of anger replacing her need to nurture him. "I just wanted to know more about you."

"Well, now you do," he said, taking her arm again to lead her into the nearly deserted restaurant. He stopped at the door. "Oh, and in answer to your other question. That meeting I had with your father yesterday? We were talking about you."

* * *

"I knew that," Autumn told Campbell after they'd ordered cheeseburgers—hers with fries and his with onion rings. "I knew you were probably talking about me. My daddy is worried about me coming back, isn't he? He doesn't think I can cut it, working for the family business, right?"

Campbell took a sip of his iced tea and marveled at the insecurity in her pretty green eyes. Did she actually think her father would kick her off the premises if she didn't work out at Maxwell Financial Group? Apparently.

Apparently, too, for all their confidence and bluster, they both had concerns regarding their places at Maxwell Financial Group. A bond that would remain between them and probably make them grow close, since they both had something to prove. *It's always about proving myself, isn't it, Lord?*

"Listen," he said, reaching out to grab one of her flailing hands. "Your father has a world of confidence in you. He is so giddy with having you home and working for him that I think it's added ten years to his life."

She looked surprised, her eyes going wide, her expression changing from scared to relaxed. "He is?"

"Of course he is," Campbell answered, still holding her hand because, well, it just felt good to hold her hand.

She realized he still had it and yanked it away, a frown on her face. "Then why the secret meeting? Why didn't he just tell me those things?"

"Hasn't he tried?"

"Well, yes, I guess he has. We talk every night before bed. I give him a summary of our day, he tells me about his golf game and his charity obligations and we kiss each other good-night and go our separate ways."

"Sounds charming."

"It's our little ritual, thank you very much."

"I like little rituals," he responded, watching as a soft blush covered her porcelain skin.

"So, this weekly meeting thing with you and my father, is that going to be a ritual?"

"If I know your father, probably so."

"But you said you talked about me. Why would my daddy want to talk to you about me?" She stopped, put a hand to her mouth, her blush turning a deep pink now. "Oh, no, he didn't give you the son-I-might-have-to-hurt-you speech, did he?"

Campbell couldn't help but smile at the exaggerated John Wayne tone in her voice. "He did. But don't go getting all worked up about it. I would do the same, in his place."

Autumn put her head in her hands. "I'm so embarrassed. Campbell, I'm almost thirty years old. I've dated all kind of scoundrels in New York—and thankfully, he didn't know about most of them—so I thought he was over that particular speech."

"He loves you. And he wants to protect you. You should be glad you have such loving parents."

She looked up then, and apologized yet again. "I'm sorry. I didn't mean to sound ungrateful. I am glad I have such a solid family, believe me. But I sure wish my daddy hadn't threatened to shoot you first and ask questions later."

"Oh, it wasn't so much a threat as a promise," he replied, winking at her. "Hey, it's okay. I have assured him that I have very honorable intentions toward you. I told him we have a very strict business agreement."

"What if he finds out we had dinner together?"

"At the Busy Burger? Please, give me some credit. If you and I were on a real date, I can assure you it wouldn't be happening at the most run-down but best burger joint in East Texas."

That brought a smile to her face, causing the dingy, dim room instantly to light up a watt or two. "And just where does a ladies' man like you take a woman on a real date?"

He looked up, pursing his lips. "Well, if we were back in Louisiana, I'd take you to Commander's Palace in the Garden District in New Orleans. Or maybe Brennan's down in the Quarter. Even my mother would approve of those two choices."

"Name-dropper," she teased. "But I love both those places. Highly romantic and quite impressive."

"Yes, and very intimate atmospheres, a lot of ambiance."

"Not like the Busy Burger," she said as rowdy laughter echoed from the next booth.

"No, nothing like this place. But then, romance depends on the company, I believe. I know of other places in the Big Easy, less famous and far less impressive but equally as good. Maybe I'd just take you to one of those, since you obviously aren't moved by prestige and name-dropping."

Autumn glanced around. Campbell watched as she took in the dusty faded blues and yellows of the plastic flowers, the wall full of wrinkled photographs and drooping dime-store paintings and the old corkboard full of battered, aged business cards.

"I'm sorry," he said. "This place looks scary and sad, but the food is incredible."

"I've seen worse," she replied, laughing. "And right now, I'm too hungry to be worried about the decor."

Campbell laughed, too. And enjoyed the way her eyes widened when Rita brought their burgers.

"Campbell, haven't seen you in a while, suga'," the skinny redhead said, smiling over at Autumn through her tortoiseshell glasses. "And I've never known you to bring a date out to our humble establishment."

Campbell bit into a juicy onion ring, then grinned. "I've never had a good reason to bring a date here before, my lovely Rita."

"I see," Rita said, wiping away a imaginary spot on the cracked table. "Must be one special woman." She grinned at Autumn, then whirled to pick up her next order at the counter running the length of the diner.

Campbell looked across at Autumn.

"You are one special woman," he said. "And I promised your father I wouldn't ever hurt you."

Autumn chewed on a fry, then leaned toward him. "I don't think we need to worry about that."

Campbell sat back to stare at her, taking in the burnished curls surrounding her face, taking in the sincere trust brimming in her eyes. "No, but I didn't exactly promise him I wouldn't fall for you, either. Because that's a promise I don't think I'm going to be able to keep."

Chapter Six

Autumn listened to the familiar hum of her laptop. She'd left Campbell hours ago, and even though she was exhausted, she couldn't seem to go to sleep. So here she sat in bed, staring at a blank e-mail screen.

She glanced around the familiar length of her spacious bedroom. It looked like something out of *Gone with the Wind,* because of her mother's efforts to preserve the integrity and history of their home. Her parents had bought this antebellum house when Autumn was a baby. It was the only home she'd ever known before college and New York. This rambling white-columned house was a historic part of Atlanta's colorful history and her mother had worked diligently to help keep that history alive.

Autumn wondered how her mother did it. How did Gayle Maxwell keep all the balls in the air? Besides keeping this wonderful old house in tip-top shape, Gayle was also a member of the Art League; the Women's Club; the Blue Ladies, who volunteered at the area hospital; the Cancer Society and the Genealogical Society and Historical Commission, not to mention the Daughters of the Republic of Texas and Friends of the Public Library. And that was just when she wasn't working down at the church Autumn had attended all her life.

"How do our mothers do it?" she typed into the e-mail.

I was just sitting here, unable to sleep because, well, because Campbell and I had dinner at the Busy Burger. Well, not exactly dinner, more like a calorie-fest. And he told me that he couldn't promise my daddy he wouldn't fall for me. But he has noble intentions. We're trying to be professional.

Anyway, I was sitting here thinking about what he told me about his life— father left when he was young, mother divorced his father and remarried back into the upper-crust society she left behind because of getting pregnant with Campbell. I thought about all that Campbell had to overcome and then I thought about my life—our lives growing up as Maxwells. We had such fairy-tale lives, didn't we? We had everything we could ask for and more, because our parents taught us never to take our wealth for granted and always to give back to our churches and our communities. Isn't it amazing that even in the Big Apple we managed to keep our small-town values?

I guess hearing about Campbell's struggle has made me think about how blessed I am. I love this house that my parents so lovingly restored. I love driving across E. Main and Hiram streets and remembering how beautiful life here in Atlanta was when I was growing up. Campbell grew up on a bayou in south Louisiana and even though he didn't tell me everything, I think he had a very tough life because his mother's family didn't acknowledge him in any way. He told me he'd been lost, but now he was safe here in Atlanta. I think he means spiritually. He's safe in God's care and he's found a place to call home. Now *I* don't feel so safe when I'm around him.

This being professional is going to be a test of my restraint and self-control. Maybe coming back to work for my daddy was a bad idea. I love the work and I'm happy here with the more relaxed atmosphere. It's almost like a rest. But having Campbell just across the hall each day is only replacing the stress I felt in New York. What am I to do? I need advice, girls. I'm slipping. But I have to be careful. Daddy has already given Campbell "the speech." Campbell told my daddy he would never hurt me. But I think he has the ability to do just that.

Autumn signed off then closed her laptop. Her curious cousins would get a kick out of that juicy e-mail, since she'd opened up and told them her innermost feelings for Campbell. But Autumn knew her cousins would give her all sorts of advice and help her to stay sane through all of this, no matter the outcome.

And just what do you expect as far as the outcome? she wondered. She'd come home with one goal—to work for her father until she could decide what else to do. Now that goal had shifted to protecting her father's company and maybe sticking around for longer than she had planned. Because of Campbell Dupree. She'd started out not trusting him, not wanting to work with him. She'd started out with a solid resentment of his presence here. Now things were changing all the way around. She was certainly beginning to trust Campbell, business-wise.

"That's the good news," she mumbled

to herself. "The bad news—I'm afraid I might be getting too close to my business partner. I don't know if I can trust him, heart-wise."

Such a predicament. How would it all turn out?

Reaching for the white Bible her mother had given her when she'd been confirmed at church, Autumn searched for words of comfort and encouragement there in the gold-edged pages. She flipped through, landing in Proverbs.

Then her eyes hit on a passage that gave her courage even while she felt goose bumps rising along her arms.

"The name of the Lord is a strong tower; the righteous run to it and are safe." Proverbs 18:10

Safe.

Campbell had needed to feel secure and safe. That was probably why he worked to help other people with their finances. He'd turned to making money and helping others with their money, because he'd been so impoverished as a child. He'd somehow turned back to God to find his strength, because deep down inside he knew his grandfather was right. Campbell needed God to help him feel secure, to help him feel safe.

"I need to feel that, too, Lord," Autumn declared. "I need to feel safe."

She turned out the lights and lay looking at the soft moon rays slanting through the white sheers of the tall, narrow windows of her bedroom. "Maybe that's what coming home is all about. Feeling safe. Maybe that's what having faith is all about—feeling safe no matter what happens."

Autumn held to that thought and finally drifted off to sleep.

He couldn't sleep.

Campbell twisted around to glare at the digital clock sitting like a laughing clown on his nightstand.

"Big day tomorrow," he reminded himself, wondering how he'd function at their investment seminar if he was all bleary-eyed and disoriented. "Blame it on that half-pound hamburger I ate tonight," he told himself. His ultrasensitive stomach was aching as if a raging-hot poker had seared its lining.

But it wasn't just the meal he'd eaten. His discomfort came as much from the company he'd shared during the meal.

Autumn Maxwell. She was so like the season she'd been born in and named after. She was all golden and warm at times, but then at other times she was as dry and brisk as fallen leaves. And Campbell really didn't know how he was going to resist her.

"How will this all turn out, Lord?" he asked, hoping God would hear his pleas for understanding.

He finally got up to get a drink of water from the bathroom next to his bedroom. Maybe he should go over his presentation for tomorrow once again. He switched on the bedside light, his gaze falling across the aged black leather Bible that had belonged to his grandfather. Marlin Dupree had always believed that insomnia could be cured by reading the Bible. Campbell decided to give it a try.

He thumbed through the pages, taking in passages here and there. Then he settled on Proverbs. "Trust in the Lord with all your heart and lean not on your own understanding." Proverbs 3:5

Trust in the Lord. Campbell had always been a self-reliant person, trusting no one but himself to make sure he was secure. He'd been poor, but he'd managed to pull himself up out of that poverty. He'd been down, but now he was on top of the world. And he'd had to turn to the Lord in order to realize that he'd never been in control, really. He'd learned that one didn't have to understand the way of faith in order to accept that faith was full of understanding.

"I need that understanding now, Lord," he said into the gray-washed night. "I need Your strength and Your assurance."

He'd promised Autumn's father he wouldn't hurt her.

But no one had promised Campbell he wouldn't be the one to get hurt.

"Another test?" he asked, lifting his gaze upward.

Maybe so. Yet another hurdle to get

over in order to find that security he'd always craved. Campbell wondered if he could pass this particular test.

Because already, he could feel the pull of Autumn's prim persuasion. Already, he both dreaded and anticipated being near her every day. Already, he could feel the security of his tired heart cracking open just a notch to let in the light of her nearness.

He didn't go back to bed for a very long time. He just sat in the chair by his bed and stared into the shadows falling across the room, his grandfather's Bible warm and heavy in his lap.

He held on to that Bible and tried to remember all the reasons he should stay away from Autumn Maxwell. But all the reasons he wanted to be *with* her kept slashing through the darkness, like white moonlight rippling over mysterious, dark waters.

"So, develop a sound financial plan and stick with it."

Autumn finished her portion of the presentation and waited for questions before Campbell stepped up to the podium.

They'd had a good turnout of around forty people. Not bad for a small-town investment firm. Of course, they'd sent mailers to all the surrounding counties, too. There were a lot of rural communities in East Texas and all of those small communities had people who needed advice with their finances. Autumn hoped the people in this room tonight would trust Maxwell Financial Group with their assets. Her father had a reputation for being reliable and honest. She aimed to see that his legacy continued for many generations to come.

"Surely someone has a question for me," she said, smiling. "Or did I bore all of you to tears?"

One gray-haired man from the back of the room raised his hand. Autumn nodded toward him. "Yes, Mr. Sledge?"

"You're too pretty to be so smart," Mr. Sledge said, then laughed along with everyone else. "But I do have a question for you."

"Of course," Autumn said, blushing as Campbell gave her an appraising look.

"What about fixed-income investments and Medicare? I'm on a tight income since I retired. I worry about my estate. Don't know if I'll have anything left for my children."

Autumn relaxed and ignored Campbell's penetrating eyes. "That *is* a tough one. But we can set you up with a long-term portfolio that includes a diversified but conservative savings and investment plan. We'd be able to rebalance your investments—shift funds from one investment account to another to keep your money secure. That way, we can avoid unnecessary risks and keep all your long-term investments under control. Plus, you'd have money set aside for any medical emergencies that might arise."

Mr. Sledge waved a hand. "I think I understand. But I'm sure you'd be willing to explain it to me all over again if I set up an appointment with you two at your office?"

"Yes, we would," Autumn said, grinning

as her daddy winked at her from his spot by the door of the conference room. "We'd love to work with you, Mr. Sledge. And we'll try to make sure you have money left over for your children."

"Fair enough," Mr. Sledge said, nodding his approval.

Campbell smiled and stepped up to the mike. "Now let's talk about the different types of investment accounts. You have stocks and bonds, mutual funds, annuities and a whole host of other possibilities. Let's go over a few of the more conservative stock options."

Autumn sat down next to her father, then glanced over at him.

"Good job," he mouthed, smiling at her.

She nodded, then turned back to listen to Campbell. His self-assurance and confidence practically poured from his bones. How had he become that way? she wondered. He'd obviously been ruthless at one time to have made it so far in the world of finance. But now, he seemed mellow and gentle. She had to wonder about the man he'd been before. Would he go back to being cutthroat and arrogant, the way he'd described himself at times, as they worked side by side? Or would he stay this way?

Autumn listened to his presentation, thinking he would surely win over even more new clients for them. She had to believe that he was sincere in wanting to help people, especially senior citizens, watch their investments and make the right choices.

"He's a good man," Richard whispered in her ear, as if reading her mind. "You know I wouldn't have hired him if he weren't." Then he leaned close. "He came highly recommended from a friend of mine down in New Orleans. He told me Campbell was a hard worker, in spite of his health problems."

"He had health problems?" Autumn asked, surprised.

"The man worked himself up a big, ugly ulcer. Nearly killed him. That's why he drinks so much milk all the time."

"And that's why he has to have so much cream in his coffee," Autumn whispered, a new kind of sensation coursing through her system. It was called being protective. She wanted to protect Campbell from any kind of pain.

"He's fine now, honey," her father told her. "He's found a good compromise."

Autumn nodded, smiled. "I know, Daddy. I think everything is going to work out for all of us."

Richard gave her a shrewd look, then leaned back in his chair. "Time will tell on that, sugar. Time will tell."

Autumn turned her attention back to Campbell. But she wasn't listening to his words. Instead, she was listening to the swift beating of her own heart. Who knew that a man talking about the NASDAQ and a buy-and-hold investment strategy could be so appealing and attractive?

Autumn had always loved numbers. It only made sense that she could easily love a man who felt the same way.

Too easily, she reminded herself as she straightened up and tried to concentrate so she wouldn't miss her next turn at the podium. Campbell finished explaining how investment accounts worked, then, after another lively round of questions, turned things back over to her.

Autumn sailed through life insurance and estate planning, intent on ending the session on a positive note. The afternoon had gone by so quickly, but then, in spite of her growing awareness of Campbell, she did enjoy discussing money issues with other people.

"I can't believe we did it," she said to her father and Campbell as they waved goodbye to the last of the attendees.

"We sure did." Campbell smiled at her, his eyes so warm and full of promise that Autumn felt little chills of anticipation moving rapidly down her spine. "I'm starving," he announced, then he glanced toward the door. "We still have a client here."

Autumn looked toward the exit. "Mrs. Mitchell, is there something else we can help you with?"

The older woman seemed unsure. "I need some advice, but I don't quite know how to go about explaining it to y'all."

Richard and Campbell walked over to join them. Richard took Mrs. Mitchell's hand in his. "Now, Betsy, you know we have a long-standing agreement. I promised George I'd take care of you."

"I know, I know," Betsy Mitchell replied, "but I don't want to take advantage. If I could just come by the office tomorrow and explain."

"Of course you can," Autumn said, sending her father and Campbell a concerned look. "How about first thing in the morning?"

"I'll be there," Mrs. Mitchell said. "Thank you all so much for this wonderful seminar. I've learned so much. And I do need some advice."

"Good, good," Richard said, patting her hand. "You come by tomorrow and we'll fix you right up. And don't worry about our fees right now. Don't worry at all."

"Thank you," the woman said, seeming relieved.

"That was strange," Campbell replied after she'd left. "I mean, did she seem distressed about something?"

"I noticed that, too," Autumn said as they gathered up their papers and handouts. "I hope she's okay. The Mitchells have been friends of my family for many, many years. That's why Daddy never sends her a bill, even though she has assets that would impress anyone. Her husband left her a vast estate." Then she glanced over at Campbell. "How do you feel about doing gratis work?"

Campbell looked affronted. "I'm not so greedy that I don't occasionally help someone out of a jam, Autumn."

"Okay, just wanted to be clear on that."

"All clear," he replied. "I know things are done differently here. Not like New Orleans, or, let's see, New York."

"Okay, point taken," she shot back. "But I did my share of volunteering at the Y with Summer. I didn't have a choice with her strong-arming me, but I would have done it anyway. You'd be amazed at how clueless some people are about money."

"Especially when they don't have any," Campbell finished.

"Exactly." Autumn knew she'd struck that nerve again. She'd hit on that dark spot where Campbell hid all his insecurities and his pain. "It's our job to correct that," she said, hoping to remind him of all he'd accomplished today.

"Did somebody mention food?" Richard called from the back of the room. "I just talked to your mother, Autumn. She's given me strict orders to bring all of us home for a good hot meal. And I do mean all of us. She specifically asked that Campbell join us."

Autumn turned to Campbell. "My mother is a great cook."

"I know. I've had one or two of her meals."

"Do you think—"

"Do you mind—"

They both stopped, then smiled at each other. "You first," Autumn said, looking down at the table.

"I was going to say, do you mind if I join you and your parents? I won't if you feel uncomfortable."

"Why would I feel uncomfortable?"

Autumn shot back. "It's just dinner, after all. With my parents."

Campbell straightened. "Oh, right. With your daddy right there, watching over us."

"More like watching our every move."

"Okay, then. So actually, I might wind up being the uncomfortable one. As in, the one skewered to the barbecue pit."

"Not if you keep it all in perspective. Just coworkers celebrating after a job well done."

"Exactly. That's all. No big deal."

"No big deal at all."

"Are you in, Campbell?" Richard said as he came to the front of the room.

"Yes, count me in," Campbell replied, his eyes on Autumn. "I appreciate the invitation and I'm hungry, too."

Autumn looked up at him, thinking she had suddenly lost her appetite. Her throat was parched and she found it hard to swallow or find her next breath. She might not be hungry, but she sure was thirsty. Again.

"Ready to get going?" her father asked, a twinkle in his eyes.

"Sure."

She walked ahead of Campbell and her father, and felt Campbell's eyes on her all the way to the parking lot.

Chapter Seven

Campbell sat at his desk, staring at the fist-sized bronze pelican that served as a paperweight. It also served as a reminder of who he was, and where he'd come from. His grandfather had given it to him one Christmas long ago.

His grandfather's words called out to Campbell. "*Allez avec Dieu.* Always go with God, Campbell."

"I hear you, *Grand-père*," Campbell said, picking up the paperweight to hold in his hand.

He thought about the dinner he'd shared with Autumn and her folks last night. Juicy steaks, nice baked potatoes, a fresh salad and some sort of apple cake for dessert. Both the meal and the company had been nice—more than nice. Even his finicky stomach had behaved. Everything had been perfect.

Perfect.

"What are you pondering?" Autumn asked from the door of his office, her sweet floral scent announcing her arrival.

Campbell looked up to find her in a pretty dress that fell straight down to her knees in a riotous confusion of fall colors. She wore a neat little brown sweater over the dress. The ambers and greens of her outfit only complimented the vibrant color in her eyes and her hair.

"You look like the picture of fall," Campbell said, still holding the pelican.

"And you didn't answer my question," she replied as she settled into a chair across from him, giving him his morning glimpse of her shoes. The woman had a lot of shoes.

These were high-heeled brown croco-dile-skin pumps. Campbell could only image that old croc was one happy camper now, his skin having gone for such a pretty cause. But then, knowing Autumn, they were probably fake. She didn't like hurting animals and she was much more frugal in her shopping habits than her cousins. Or so she'd told Janice one morning. And Campbell had just happened to overhear.

He lifted his eyes to her face, put down the pelican, then leaned up in his chair. "Actually, I was thinking about you."

He loved the way her cheeks flamed with a fresh pink blush. "What about me?"

"I had a very nice time last night. I'm sending your mother flowers today to thank her. Janice suggested a nice fall arrangement of mums and sunflowers."

"That's mighty sweet of you. I guess it never hurts to make nice with the boss's wife."

He saw the mirth in her eyes. "But it's very hard to make nice with the boss's daughter, right?"

"I think we're beyond that now, don't you?"

"Are we?" He placed his elbows on the

desk, then watched her. "Do you understand how much it meant to me, to be there with you and your folks last night? You have a good, solid family, Autumn. I envy that."

She looked surprised, then baffled. "But you said you had that, too, with your Cajun relatives. Did I misunderstand?"

"No, no misunderstanding. I had plenty of relatives around me, growing up. Except the two that mattered the most."

"Your parents."

He hated the softening in her eyes. He didn't want sympathy. "My parents."

She fixed her expression, changing her face into a blank canvas. He appreciated that about her. Then she picked up the tiny pelican paperweight and looked down at it. "You know, April lost her mother when she was in high school. I can't imagine going through that. On the other hand, Summer's parents traveled a lot when she was growing up. They left her with her grandparents, and she's had abandonment issues of her own to deal with. Even the best of parents make mistakes. But it must have been awful with your father running off. What I don't get is how your mother could—"

"Could conveniently forget that she had a son?"

"I don't mean to be cruel, Campbell. But that just doesn't register in my mind. I mean, Summer's parents always loved her, even if they weren't around all the time. I can't imagine a parent purposely ignoring a child."

He looked across the desk at her, seeing the sincerity in her eyes. "No, you wouldn't know about that. Your parents adore you."

"They also love me. That's what counts."

"Yes, there is that. I think my mother loved me, but she didn't know how to show me that love. She was ashamed of me, of what my father had done to both of us. So she buried her shame in work. She had to have that security in order to survive, in order to rise above our poverty, and to show her uppity folks she could handle things. When she remarried and finally had everything she could ever want, she realized she'd lost the one thing that could bring her some peace."

"Her son?"

"Her son."

"Maybe you need to really forgive your mother. Maybe if you did that, you could both find that security you seem to be missing."

"Me, I'm not missing a thing," he said, pushing back to end the uncomfortable intimacy of the conversation. He'd told her too much about himself and now her analytical mind would take that information and run with it. Why did women always think they could figure men out and fix them? "I just wanted you to know how much I appreciated last night."

Autumn got up, her expression telling him she wasn't through with him yet. "Right. Well, you know you're welcome at our home any time." Then she gave him a sharp look. "Why didn't you tell me about your ulcer?"

Campbell shrugged. "It's not very glamorous. How'd you find out?"

"My daddy told me. I think he's afraid I'll contribute to your medical condition becoming worse."

Campbell clutched his stomach. "You have caused me a few pangs."

"I don't want to do that. We need you here."

Campbell's head shot up. "Could you please repeat that? 'Cause I don't think I heard you right. Did you say you need me?"

Her blush flowed sweet and pink. "I said *we* need you—here, every day, working hard."

"Oh, I see. You don't want me keeling over in agony, since you've finally realized how brilliant I am."

She gave him a smirk of a smile. "Something like that." But he saw the sincerity in her eyes. And basked in it.

"Thanks." He glanced at his watch, squirming under her concerned scrutiny even if it did make him feel good. "I wonder if Mrs. Mitchell will make it in all right."

"It's almost nine. If she isn't here soon, I'll give her a call."

"Good idea. I pulled up her portfolio. Did you know she's been shifting some money market funds around down at the credit union?"

"No." Autumn came around the desk to read the file showing on the computer screen. "That's odd. She's moved large chunks of money into her checking account. What on earth could be going on there?"

"Maybe that's what she wants to talk to us about," Campbell said, enjoying being so near Autumn. He couldn't help but stare down at her unruly burnished curls as she leaned over his desk. He stood, still staring.

She straightened and caught him. Her eyes widened at the same time her lips parted. "Campbell?"

"Hmm?"

"Can I get by, please? I think I heard someone come in."

He stepped closer. "Janice will show Mrs. Mitchell in."

Autumn lifted away. "Janice had a doctor's appointment, remember? She'll be here at 9:30."

He reluctantly retreated back into reality. "Oh, sorry."

A weak voice called out, "Anyone here?"

"We're in here, Mrs. Mitchell," Autumn answered as she hopped around the desk and fluffed her hair.

Okay, Campbell told himself, time to put on your professional face. Don't think about family dinners and a woman who could easily change you for the better. Just think about your job and your own peace of mind.

Campbell reminded himself why he was here. And it wasn't to fall for Autumn Maxwell. Work. He needed to concentrate on work. Maybe he was more like his mother than he'd realized. Work was still his salvation.

He waited as Autumn ushered frail Betsy Mitchell into the room. The woman looked at him as if he might bite her. She seemed very upset and nervous.

"Have a seat, Mrs. Mitchell," he said, recovering both his composure and his confidence. "Now, how can we help you?"

Betsy Mitchell sank into a chair and clutched it with both hands, her wrinkled knuckles going white. "I think I've made a terrible mistake."

"What's wrong?" Autumn asked, sitting down across from the older woman. "What do you mean?"

Tears formed in Mrs. Mitchell's hazel eyes. "I think I've become involved with a...a con man."

"A con man?"

Richard looked from Autumn to Campbell, his anger apparent in the frown on his face, and in the way his voice grew louder with each pointed question. "Would either of you like to explain to me how you let this happen? Do I need to remind you that the Mitchells have been clients of ours since the opening of this firm? Did either of you even check this out? Or when was the last time either of you checked on Betsy's finances? This beats the Alamo! This is bigger than the Rio Grande! Who's going to give me some answers?"

"Daddy, sit down," Autumn said, closing the door so poor distraught Mrs. Mitchell wouldn't hear her father's rage. "We called you down here because we need your advice on this. Janice just came in and she's with Miss Betsy now, giving her a nice cup of tea."

"Tea?" Richard slid onto a chair. "Hogwash and corned beef hash, Autumn. You called me all in a tizzy about this. Tea won't help the fact that the woman has lost thousands of dollars to some sweet-talking, two-timing drifter who knew exactly what buttons to push to get to her money, and exactly which bank accounts to hack into, I might add."

Campbell motioned to Autumn, then cleared his throat. "I take full responsibility, Richard. I did try to get in touch with Mrs. Mitchell when I first came aboard, but she kept assuring me that she was fine, financially. She insisted we just back off and let her handle her own finances.

Then she told me she was going to do some traveling—"

"With that con man, no doubt!"

"Yes, I'm sure that's what happened—" Autumn started, only to shut up when her father stared her down. "Daddy," she finally said, giving him back a look that echoed his own and made Campbell smile in spite of the seriousness of the situation, "we can only *advise* our clients. We can't make them hold on to their money. Mrs. Mitchell didn't come to us with this because, well, because she trusted this man. He convinced her to make these transactions on her own, without our advice, and then he started taking money without her knowledge. She thought he really cared about her."

"She's been alone and very vulnerable since her husband's death," Campbell finished, his eyes connecting with Autumn's. "This man was watching and waiting and apparently he found his mark."

Richard got up, fisting his hands. "I've never let a client down. Even when the economy and the markets have been bad, I've never allowed this to happen. Betsy lost a big chunk of her life savings, everything they both worked so hard for. I can't allow this to happen."

"What can we do?" Autumn asked, her shoulders slumping as she held her hands to her stomach. She felt as if she might be the one with an ulcer.

"We can try to locate this man," Campbell offered. "We can track him down, have him arrested. Maybe recoup some of Mrs. Mitchell's money."

"You'd be willing to do that?" Autumn asked, her voice quivering.

"Of course I would," Campbell said, nodding. "I used to be ruthless and inscrutable, remember? It takes a good con to know another one."

"We don't need any more trouble, son," Richard said, holding up a hand. "We don't need you going to jail."

"I won't do anything illegal," Campbell replied. "But I will find this man and bring him back. I owe Mrs. Mitchell that much, at least."

"I'll help you," Autumn blurted, her eyes widening. "Whatever it takes."

Richard shook his head. "Now, hold on just a minute. We need to let the authorities know about this man."

"Mrs. Mitchell is too embarrassed to press charges, Daddy. She doesn't want anyone else to find out about this."

"Well, if that don't beat all. Well, Betsy is a proud woman."

Campbell stood up, his hands in the air. "Richard, let me handle this before we bring in the authorities. We can keep it quiet for Mrs. Mitchell's sake."

"But what if we only make things worse?" Autumn asked, her expression doubtful.

"It can't get any worse," Campbell replied. "This man is probably long gone by now, but we have to try. Look, it's risky, I know, but I'd rather go after this man myself, not only to protect Mrs. Mitchell, but also this firm. Just give me a couple of days, Richard. If I can't find anything out, then we'll go to the police."

Richard thought about it for a minute, then said, "I guess we could do some investigating on our own, though I still think we ought to inform the local and state authorities about this. But maybe you're right. Maybe we should take matters into our own hands, since Betsy is so skittish right now. As long as we keep it discreet and quiet." Then he gave them both a withering scowl. "But I mean it—I don't want you two getting into any trouble."

Campbell nodded. "Just two days, then I'll talk to the police and explain what's happened. We need to go about tracking down this man."

Autumn nodded. "I said I'd help. I'll do whatever needs to be done."

Campbell glanced over at her. "It might mean working extra hours."

"I don't mind."

"Are you sure?"

She gave him a look that told him he'd just insulted her. "Of course I'm sure. I want this man arrested. I can't take that pain I see in Mrs. Mitchell's eyes. She is a sweet, good-hearted woman. She doesn't deserve this."

"Okay," Campbell said, admiring Autumn

tenfold. Then he turned to Richard. "We'll get right on this, I promise."

"Good," Richard said, a sigh of relief clearing the frown off his face. "I'll go and try to comfort Betsy. At least she'll see that she's not alone in this. We'll make this right."

"Yes, we'll make it right," Campbell said, his eyes on Autumn. "Together."

She nodded, watched her father leave the room, then turned to face him. "Just what exactly did you have in mind?"

He was making it up as he went. Campbell drove his motorcycle up the long gravel lane leading to the Maxwell house, the view taking his breath away. This house reminded him of the other side of life he'd always wondered about back on the bayou. The genteel, privileged life his mother had given up in order to be with his father.

No wonder she'd found a new husband, Campbell thought, remembering long periods of no electricity and barely any running water in the tiny house they'd lived in out in the swamps. Now, he had a hard time picturing his classy, cultured mother living like that. Now, she didn't talk about those days, to anyone.

You tried, *Maman*, didn't you?

He could understand his mother's need to work day and night. He'd been the same. Still was. It was all about security and peace of mind. It was all about principles and integrity.

Maybe Autumn was right. Maybe it was time to forgive his mother—really forgive her. But right now, he and Autumn had other things to deal with. They were going to do some detective work, to find the man who'd stolen Betsy Mitchell's life savings.

Campbell couldn't wait to make the man pay.

He brought the growling bike to a halt in the middle of the circular driveway. Before he could take off his helmet, Autumn shot out the front door in jeans and a sweater, her hands on her hips.

"I'm not getting on that thing."

"Then I reckon you can walk behind."

"You didn't tell me we'd be riding around East Texas on that monster."

"You didn't ask, so I figured the mode of transportation didn't matter."

"Well, it does. We'll take my car."

"Oh, no." Campbell swung off the bike and stared up to where she stood on the steps of the front porch like Scarlett guarding Tara. "C'mon, live a little, Autumn. I'm a safe driver. And I brought you a helmet."

She eyed the bike as if it were some sort of scary creature. "We'll look so obvious."

"No, we'll look like a couple out on a lazy Saturday morning drive. This is the perfect cover."

She came down the steps, her citified black boots clicking on the asphalt walkway. "You're just saying that so you can get me on that ridiculous thing, right?"

"I'm sure you'll enjoy it if you just go with an open mind."

She shook her head. "I don't have an open mind, not when it comes to my safety. You know the statistics about these things."

"I'm a good driver," he repeated, each word slow and steady. "And we're wasting precious daylight here."

"It's only ten o'clock in the morning, Campbell."

"Yeah, well, the sun's moving in the sky, sugar. We need to make tracks if we're going to check all the places Betsy suggested we try to find…what's-his-name."

"Willard. His name is Willard Watson," Autumn said, tugging her pullover sweater down over her jeans. "Let's get this over with."

Campbell nodded, then took off his leather jacket. "Here, you'll need this."

Autumn stared at the jacket with a frown, but she finally put it on. "I could go get one from the house," she mumbled as he guided her to the bike.

"Isn't more fun to wear your boy-friend's jacket?"

"You are *not* my boyfriend."

"We have to pretend," he reminded her.

"Try to act as if you actually like being around me, okay?"

"I'll try," she said, giving him a mock smile as she crammed the bright red helmet over her head. It fell down over her eyes.

Campbell laughed, adjusted the helmet and took a minute to tuck her hair off her face. "I wouldn't have taken you for a chicken, Autumn. I can't believe you're afraid of a motorcycle."

"I'm not chicken, but I do have common sense," she replied, tossing her head and causing the helmet to shift. "And my common sense is telling me this whole amateur sleuth thing is a very bad idea."

"I can investigate this on my own," he offered, knowing she was too stubborn to allow that. "I don't want you getting in any trouble. Your daddy would have my hide."

"No, oh, no," she said, determination making her look like a schoolyard bully. "I intend to find Willard Watson and bring him to justice."

"Let's go, then," Campbell retorted as he hopped on the bike. "We've got several restaurants and church socials to cover."

Autumn climbed on the bike behind him. "I can't believe this scoundrel hung out at church gatherings."

"That's where the widows are, darlin'."

"It's wrong. It's so wrong."

Campbell looked back over his shoulder at her, enjoying being near her like this in spite of the dire circumstances of their mission. "That's where we come in. We're going to retrack ol' Willard's every step until we find out where he took off to, and we're going to find him and try to get back what we can of Betsy Mitchell's money."

Autumn looked doubtful. "Maybe we should just let the police handle this, like Daddy suggested. I know Betsy was too embarrassed to risk pressing charges, but maybe we should just report what we know and let the authorities do the rest."

"We'll convince Betsy to press charges if we can't find anything on our own. But we can take things a few steps further than our local boys can by inquiring on our own, and maybe we'll save Mrs. Mitchell that humiliation if we can get to this man first."

"I don't think Daddy was happy with doing it this way," she reminded him.

"He'll be fine with it as long as we don't do anything too heroic or stupid."

He saw the gratitude in Autumn's eyes. "I appreciate you helping with this, Campbell, even if I do think it's too risky."

"It's my job, my responsibility. I should have been more aware of Betsy's situation."

Autumn touched a hand to his arm. "This man took advantage of her, Campbell. He played on her loneliness and her emotions. That's a worse crime than taking her money, in my book."

Campbell felt the warmth of her touch even while he saw the censure in her eyes, and wondered if Autumn was sending him a not-so-subtle warning. *She* wasn't a woman to be messed with, that was for sure. And he wasn't so reckless and carefree that he'd trample on her heart.

But he sure wanted to win over that common-sense attitude and very fragile heart of hers.

"We'll get to the bottom of this, I promise," he told her. Then he sat there wondering how he was going to actually keep that promise.

Finally, she poked him in the ribs. "Hey, crank this bad boy up. We've got work to do."

Campbell grinned in spite of his worries. One thing was certain. Life with Autumn Maxwell would never be dull. In fact, working with this woman might turn out to be the most daring thing he'd ever tried.

Chapter Eight

"Why are we here?" Autumn asked Campbell a half hour later as she glanced around the Busy Burger. "I thought after I visited with Betsy and gathered information yesterday, we were going to talk to the people from her Sunday school class who might know more about this Willard person."

"We are," Campbell replied, his fingers tapping a nervous beat on the aged table. "I needed some pie and coffee first."

Autumn let out an impatient sigh. "Pie and coffee? You needed pie and coffee, after hurrying me? Who eats pie this early in the morning?"

"I do," he replied, his tone and demeanor making her want to order a whole pie to throw in his face. "And if you'll just relax, I'll explain why I stopped here first."

"I'm all ears," she said, her smile as fake as the plastic daisies in the Mason jar on their table. "But I don't get it. You were all gung ho to get going on this. We agreed I'd keep in touch with Betsy, and you'd follow up on any information we found. Or that we'd follow up together. Are you having second thoughts about me coming along?"

"No, no second thoughts. I just wanted some time with you, to make sure you understand things. We have to be very careful."

"I know that, Campbell. You and my father have both preached that to me."

"Okay then, open that pretty mind of yours and listen good," Campbell told her as he took a huge bite of his apple pie. "Before you turn into Nancy Drew, there are a few ground rules we need to establish."

Autumn took a drink of her orange juice and nodded. "Such as?"

"Such as, this type of thing is all about human nature. This man came into Betsy's life when she was lonely—a brand-new widow. That's a fact. He watched and waited for just the right mark. He did it by listening and by asking the right questions. He did it by being in the right places at the right times. He took full advantage of all situations and then he skipped town with a lot of Betsy's money. So that is exactly how I aim to catch him—by taking advantage of all situations."

Autumn had to admire the determined look on his face, even if he was shoveling in pie and intrigue with each word. "Okay, I'm listening now. Keep talking."

"How good are you at gossiping?" he asked, his expression so serious she almost burst out laughing.

But this was no laughing matter. "I guess I'm okay at it. I mean, I gossip with my cousins about family things and we used to gossip about friends and co-workers back in New York. I try not to be malicious."

He shot her a broad killer grin. "I can't imagine you being malicious, no."

"So why should I be so adept at gossip, then?"

"Because we need to listen to any and all gossip we can hear—at both this church social this afternoon and any other place Willard might have hung around. It's amazing the wealth of information you can gather if you just look and listen and let people talk."

"But won't that be considered hearsay if we present it to the authorities?"

"Technically, it would be if a cop depended on it for an official statement. It would have to be proven in court. But we're not cops. We're just two very concerned citizens. The rules don't necessarily apply to us. As long as we don't get caught breaking and entering, we don't need a warrant for a search and we don't have to worry about entrapment. We can make the rules up as we go."

"Well, thanks for explaining that to me, Mr. Hardy Boy. Not that I plan on breaking any laws, however."

He lifted an eyebrow. "Hardy Boy?"

"If I'm Nancy Drew, then that makes you—"

"Very funny." He finished off the pie in record time. "Just consider it said—I've warned you. We might have to break some rules to find dashing Willard."

She picked at her napkin, then glared across the table at him. "And just for the record, I like living by the rules. Rules keep us out of hot water. So I repeat, I don't intend to do any breaking and entering, or anything else underhanded and crooked, period."

"Well, I hope we won't have to," he replied. "But let's get back on task. Here's some more information for you. If you're talking to someone and their mannerism seems to change suddenly, that's a red flag that they probably know something they're not saying."

"How will *I* be able to tell?" she asked, fascinated that he seemed to know so much about criminals. And concerned that he could tell exactly when her own mannerisms suddenly changed each time she was near him.

He leaned in and whispered, "They might start blinking or fidgeting. They won't make eye contact with you. They might go from relaxed to nervous in record time."

Autumn sat straight up in her chair. "I've done that very thing myself before, when I've been uncomfortable."

He grinned. "I know. I've seen you in action."

So he did watch for things like that! That just figured. Autumn thought the more she knew about Campbell Dupree, the less she actually understood him. She didn't even want to think about what he might read into her erratic actions. So she went back to task as he had suggested. "But I'm certainly not a criminal."

"No, but we all hold back, have something to hide at times. It's just part of being human."

The look he gave her made her want to fidget right now, but she willed herself to sit still and look directly into his intense dark eyes. This lasted about five seconds, before she grabbed her juice and drained the glass.

Campbell touched her hand. "We have to go on intuition sometimes, Autumn."

"Intuition?" Her intuition was telling her that this was another fine mess she'd gotten herself into. "You mean, when we're snooping around?"

He refused to let go of her hand. "That, and with other things."

He didn't have to tell her which other things. Why was it so hard to sit here and look across this booth at the man? Maybe because her entire being was so in tune with him?

"Got it," she finally said, pulling her hand away to grab her petite leather backpack. "Thanks for the 411 on criminal investigations. Now, let's go."

Campbell took her hand again, bringing her back to her seat, his eyes sweeping her with a pleading look. "It's important that you take my instructions seriously. I don't want anything to happen to you. I want to keep you safe."

That statement stilled her, except for

the crush of her heart beating to escape. "You want to keep the entire world safe, I think."

"No, just you and me today, darlin'. And the Betsy Mitchells of this world."

Why did he always have to go and say something so incredibly sweet and heroic, just when she was doubting him the most? "It sounds as if you've done this sort of thing before."

"I've had clients who've gotten into trouble before. So I've learned a few tricks along the way."

The look in his dark eyes caused Autumn's heart to do little flips and rolls. There was an alluring danger to this man. But the paradox of that danger was that Autumn did feel completely safe with him. It was a good kind of danger, the kind that heroes faced and accepted, the kind that brought out integrity and courage, the kind that made a woman think she could easily fall in love sitting in a greasy spoon watching a man eat apple pie.

It was also the kind of delicious danger

that could get her in a whole peck of trouble. So she prayed that her own instincts and woman's intuition were steering her onto the right path. She prayed that God would be on that path with her, guiding her.

"I understand," she said, trying very hard not to alarm Campbell with her total devotion just yet. "I'm a big girl, Campbell. I've lived in a big, bad city for years now, remember? I can take care of myself."

He leaned forward again, his eyes rich with secrets and promises. "Do you actually think bad things only happen in the big city, Autumn? Human nature is the same, no matter the per capita ratio, no matter the population. Evil is everywhere in this old world."

"Now you *are* scaring me," she said, highly aware of the warmth of his hand on her arm. "Let's just go and get this started. We're wasting time here. I know the drill and I'll…I'll try to follow your lead."

He got up, threw a ten on the table, then

waved to their waitress. "Now that was worth the trip."

"What?" Autumn asked as he held the rickety door for her.

He stood still, looking down at her. "Having you say you'll follow my lead."

"Don't get used to it," she replied with a toss of her hair, leaving him standing there. "And don't let that door hit you on your way out."

They approached the small country church as if it were a den of gangsters. "Remember," Campbell said through a pleasant smile, "we're here to listen and learn."

"I don't want to lie or pretend," Autumn replied as they headed for the attached fellowship hall where the monthly seniors' social was supposed to be taking place.

According to Mrs. Mitchell, this was a popular get-together for the widows and widowers of the church. That's how she'd met Willard Watson.

April remembered Betsy's distraught words to her yesterday. "He was so nice, so polite and charming. He made me feel young again. He talked about all these grand plans. I thought he was a true Southern gentleman."

How could a man do that to a woman? How could this have happened to someone as good and decent as Betsy Mitchell? Maybe because she was good and decent, and very vulnerable.

"We don't have to lie," Campbell said, bringing Autumn back to the present. "We're here because we know Betsy and we wanted to thank everyone for helping her through a difficult time. She's not feeling well—that much is true. Then we just sit back and let the good times roll."

"There is nothing good about this."

"Work with me, sweetheart," Campbell said in his best Humphrey Bogart voice. "Be a good girl and I'll take you for a long ride on my bike and an even longer dinner at a legitimate, candlelit restaurant."

"You really know how to turn a girl's head," Autumn retorted, but he heard the amusement in her voice.

Campbell breathed a sigh of relief. He

needed her relaxed and loose in order to pull this off. He didn't want to be deceitful, so he had to walk a fine line between being truthful with this endearing group and pulling his own con on them. Autumn wouldn't go for any sort of con, so he aimed to be up-front. And he prayed they'd get some answers.

"You ready?" he asked her as they stood just outside the open door, the laughter and chatter from inside floating out over the beautiful fall afternoon.

"Sure," she said, glancing down at the barrel of colorful orange and burgundy mums sitting by the door. "I'm always ready to strong-arm a few unwitting senior citizens."

"Just—"

"I know, I know. Just follow your lead."

"You're learning."

"Only because I want to get that man off the streets and out of the churches and fellowship halls."

"There's the spirit."

Campbell took her hand and pulled her with him inside the long, narrow building.

They were immediately met with greet-ings from all corners.

"Well, hello there," a diminutive woman with gray-blond spiked hair said from a table positioned by the door. "My, my, we don't usually get 'em as young as you two. Surely you're not…a widow and a widower, are you?"

"No, ma'am," Campbell said, a smile in his voice. "We're good friends with Betsy Mitchell. She's a little down today—"

"I'll say," the woman, whose name badge read Martha, said with a wave of her hand. "After what that Willard did to her, I can only imagine."

"What do you mean?" Autumn asked. Campbell felt her whole body go on alert, so he had to squeeze her fingers to remind her to play it cool. "I mean, what did happen between her and Willard?" Autumn said on a much sweeter note. Then she put a hand over one side of her mouth and whispered, "I think that's why she's so down these days."

"He broke her heart, is all," Martha replied as she took their $3.50 per plate for the potluck meal. "We all had them pegged to get married right away, but Willard got called away on some sort of job a while back. Of course, Betsy hasn't seen hide nor hair of him in two weeks, and well, since he hasn't called, she's more than a little concerned. She thinks she's seen the last of him, I'm afraid. I called her yesterday to come and help with the fall rummage sale, but she was too blue to leave the house. That's not a good sign."

"Oh, my, how terrible," Autumn said, the sincerity in her voice ringing pure and true. "Miss Betsy had mentioned that he was away. We were hoping he'd be here today, so we could tell him that's she a bit under the weather."

Campbell put his wallet back in his pocket after paying for their lunch. Apparently, Betsy hadn't told Martha the whole story. "Do you know where Willard went?"

"Naw," Martha said, smiling at the next person coming through the door. "He didn't talk about his work too much.

Some of the other men might know, though."

"Thank you so much," Autumn said. "We've heard the food is really good at these socials. Betsy really wanted us to drop by and tell you all how much she appreciates all of you."

"That's mighty nice of her," Martha called as they walked into the lunch line. "Y'all be sure and stay around for the gospel quartet. Those boys can really sing."

"We look forward to it," Campbell replied. Then he turned to Autumn. "So far, so good."

"This wasn't as hard as I thought it would be," Autumn said in a tight whisper.

"We're not done yet. I don't think Betsy has told anyone that when Willard got called away, he took half her life savings with him."

"No, I don't think so, which is why we have to be very careful."

"Look and listen," Campbell reminded her, his eyes scanning the crowd. "Before we finish here today, we should have a

thorough background on one Willard
Watson."

"Probably more information than we
ever wanted to know," Autumn said,
chuckling.

"Yes, but this is just the beginning. I
intend to do a thorough search down at the
courthouse, too."

"How?"

"Public records. If he has anything so
much as a traffic ticket, it will help us.
I'm going to check at small claims court,
too. I have a distinct feeling that Willard
has probably passed his share of bad
checks."

"You continue to amaze me," Autumn
said, shock clearing her face before she
replaced it with a dainty smile. "I don't
even want to know how you learned all of
this stuff."

"Then I won't tell you. Just keep
smiling, princess. You look so natural
doing it."

"Why, thank you. And don't call me
princess."

"Let's not fight in front of the old people."

"I'm not going to fight. But I will kick you in the shin if you mess with me."

"You are one high-maintenance date."

"And don't you forget it. But we're not on a date."

"Part of our undercover cover, remember?"

"Oh, right. Okay, then I guess we are on a date, because I refuse to—"

"I know, I know. You won't stoop to being deceitful."

"That's right."

He didn't bring up the fact that they were both deceiving themselves in trying to keep things between them strictly professional. Now probably wasn't the time for that.

They both turned on smiles as yet another senior citizen introduced himself and started talking all about the courtship of Betsy and Willard. And teased Campbell and Autumn about their own obviously budding courtship.

Which neither one of them bothered to deny.

Chapter Nine

The sun was setting by the time Campbell pulled the big bike into the driveway of his house. Autumn waited, clutching his waist, as he shut off the motor then turned to her. "You looked wiped out," he said, his eyes going a soft brown.

She tugged off her helmet, then stepped off the bike, thinking she needed to distance herself from the security of being close to him. "I *am* tired."

He helped her to her feet, placing her helmet back on the seat. "We can do the rest of this tomorrow."

"No, we do it now." She started toward the cute white cottage. "I don't want to forget anything since you were right about some of the men clamming up and acting strange. They definitely started acting erratic when I questioned them too closely. I think a couple of them knew things they didn't want to speculate about. And I think I should call Daddy and give him an update."

Campbell caught up with her by the wisteria vine. "Hey, hey, hold on." He whirled her around. "Are you all right?"

Autumn wanted to scream out to him that she wasn't all right. That being forced to spend a glorious fall Saturday with him had been sheer torture, a sweet torture that only made her want to laugh and cry at the same time because she had never, ever expected her feelings to be as swift and fast-moving as a waterfall.

They'd been in several public places full of people milling around, and yet, at times she'd felt as if it were just the two of them, staring at each other across the room. In spite of all the information she'd tried to digest today, Autumn couldn't get the feel of being with Campbell out of her system.

She'd liked it way too much to push it away.

Sending up a prayer for control, she said, "I'm fine. Just tired, like I said."

He held her there, the soft golden dusk coloring him in rich hues of yellow and brown. "I really wanted us to have that long drive and a nice, quiet dinner."

"I know," she said, her imagination taking flights of fancy at just the thought of such an intimate setting. "But we've had a long day and we've worked hard. Maybe we can have that dinner after this is all over. Then I'll be in the mood to celebrate."

He wouldn't let her go. "Are you uncomfortable, being here with me?"

Autumn couldn't tell him everything in her heart. "I don't know. Maybe. We could go back to my house to use the computer in my dad's office."

He looked down at her, compassion coloring his eyes. That and some other dark emotion that she didn't want to read too closely. "Then that's what we'll do. Just let me grab a few files, okay?"

"Okay."

He hurried to the door. "You can come inside and wait if you want. I promise I'll be on my best behavior."

Autumn took a deep breath, then followed him, her gaze taking in the starkly furnished little house. The living-room area held a futon-style couch and a television. A cluttered desk holding a state-of-the-art computer system sat in one corner of the tiny kitchen where a dining table should have been. A starkly rendered painting of a lone figure guiding a pirogue through a dark bayou hung over the sealed-up fireplace.

"You don't seem to be settled yet," she said, pointing toward the various boxes stacked here and there around the combination living room and kitchen. His house looked just like his office. Unsettled, unkempt, unorganized.

"I don't intend to stay here," he said over his shoulder as he disappeared into a room down the short hall.

Autumn's heart halted at that declaration. So, the man who moved around a lot had already decided he wasn't putting down roots in tiny Atlanta, Texas? But why had he said all those things to her?

"What do you mean?" she called, surprise and disappointment causing her question to sound shrill.

He came back into the room, a briefcase under one arm and a huge manila accordion file under the other. "Oh, I'm renovating a cabin out on Caddo Lake. I'll be moving out there permanently just as soon as it's finished. Didn't I mention that to you?"

The relief that rushed through Autumn only added to her agitation. "Oh, maybe you did. That's great. Wonderful."

Campbell stepped close to her, his five o'clock shadow making him seem mysterious, the victory in his eyes making him seem smug. "You sure seem glad about that."

"I just misunderstood what you said," she replied, turning for the door. "I thought you were saying you weren't going to be staying here in Atlanta, that you'd be leaving soon or something like that." Her voice trailed off as embarrassment colored her skin.

He caught up with her as they came out onto the porch. "You don't want me to leave, do you?"

Giving him a twisted frown, she slapped his arm. "Don't make anything out of that, Campbell. I don't want you to leave my daddy in the lurch, that's for sure."

He shifted the file, a knowing look on his face. "We'll take the 'Vette this time."

Autumn followed him, wondering why he hadn't had a quick comeback for what she'd just said. The man always tried to have the last word. Now he was too quiet.

He loaded the file and briefcase into the trunk, then opened the door of the convertible for her. After watching her get inside the gleaming car, he shut the door then leaned over. "I don't plan on leaving anyone in the lurch, darlin'. Especially you."

With that he came around the car and hopped in the driver's seat. "Wonder what your mother cooked for dinner tonight."

Autumn wondered how she'd possibly get through even more hours spent with this man. None of this made any sense. He was reckless, impulsive, impossible and...adorable.

And I'm cautious, careful and practical, and so not adorable, she told herself. We don't match at all.

But as Campbell put the powerful car into gear and they took off into the gleaming Texas-sized sunset, Autumn could only imagine what being with Campbell on a permanent basis might be like.

Things certainly wouldn't be dull with a man like Campbell. Unexpected twists, impulsive side trips, surprising new revelations. Life with Campbell would be like riding a fast-moving roller coaster. It took her breath away.

But Autumn needed more. She needed security and hope and love and a firm commitment.

She'd always had to have proof of things. She'd always relied on her judgment and her intelligence to get her through life. When she stopped to think about it, in spite of being raised in a Christian family, she'd never really been tested on her faith. It was just there, inside her. Maybe she'd taken that faith for granted, knowing she'd never had to just go on faith alone before. Until now.

Now, as the wind played through her hair and the sun settled in mellow oranges and soft-hued pinks over the Texas sky, she had to wonder if maybe it wasn't time to take a very big leap of faith.

"Okay, so let's go over everything we've learned so far," Campbell said to her a couple of hours later.

They'd had dinner with her parents and were in her father's roomy paneled study, loading information into the computer for the file they were building on Willard Watson. After being filled in, Richard had wanted to "help" them, but thankfully, Gayle had steered him to the other side of the house to watch a movie with her.

Autumn had finished keying in most of what they'd found on their mission today.

She leaned back in the squeaky leather chair that reminded her of sitting here in her father's lap when she'd been little, fascinated by all his notebooks and ledger sheets.

Pushing those memories away, she said, "Let's see. Betsy Mitchell met Willard Watson at the widows and widowers church social about three months ago. They hit it off just right, according to our friend Martha. We verified that with just about everyone we talked to today. Of course, we also verified that Willard seemed too good to be true at times, too. Some of the men today seemed a bit put off by all his charm and his know-it-all attitude. But not enough to open up to us, unfortunately."

Campbell settled back against a massive oak table, his eyes scanning the computer screen. "All of our sources point to one thing. Willard went after Betsy with all the zeal of a man smitten."

"Yes, smitten with her substantial bank account," Autumn said, disgust evident in her words. "But then, we'd already figured all of this out. We really didn't learn anything new today, at least not anything concrete that can help us track him down." She shrugged. "While some of the people we talked to had their suspicions, that alone won't hold up enough to build a case. We need Betsy to step forward and go after this man. It's the only way."

Campbell drained his coffee. "Well, we know he's probably headed south, maybe to Mexico or South America. He has to hide out awhile until this blows over. Maybe we can convince Betsy to take action before it's too late."

"You want more coffee?" she asked, hopping up to grab his empty cup.

He held her arm. "No, I'm still full from your mother's beef stew and biscuits. I think I'm in love."

Autumn's heart did that little thing, that little twitching thing that made her so aware of being near him. To hide that, she played along with him. "You're in love with my mother?"

"I might be. Only she's older than me

and taken." His smile was sheer entice-
ment. "That leaves her very pretty daughter.
Can you cook?"

"No," she said, slipping back down in
the chair, her knees going weak. "I'm
more of a sandwich, salad or takeout kind
of woman. Too bad."

"Yes, too bad. I thought this might be
the beginning of a beautiful relationship."

"You really watch too many old
movies, you know."

"Maybe I'm a hopeless romantic at
heart."

She didn't dare look at him. "Shouldn't
we get back to the task at hand, a romance
that went bad because this scoundrel, bad
man, ran off with Miss Betsy's money?"

He whirled her chair around so fast, her
head was spinning right along with her
heart. "You're so cute when you're calling
people names." Then he turned serious.
"We know what Willard did. We've talked
to enough people to know exactly how he
played it. He sweet-talked a lonely widow
and she gave him information that she
shouldn't have given him. He convinced

her that he could help double her finances, so she let him see her private records and the numbers in her bank account. Then he wiped her out and left her high and dry."

"From what we heard at that last restaurant, that was his modus operandi. He's probably left a few other women reeling, too." She looked down at her hands. "I can't believe he took all of them to the same places, plying them with dinner and flowers. Did he think no one would notice? It sounds as if he had special places for just this type of thing, from what that hostess told us."

"Yes, the man had his game down pat, and we're lucky that someone did notice." Campbell still held his hands on the chair, his eyes moving over Autumn's face. "Now we have to prove all of this. We have to dig into files and find some way to nail this...."

He didn't finish. Instead he leaned down and looked into Autumn's eyes. She looked up, holding his gaze, her heart hammering a beat that matched the clanging strokes of the grandfather clock out in the hallway. "What are you doing?"

Campbell's smile was soft and sweet, breathtaking in its confidence. "I'm tired of talking about Willard. I was tired of talking about Willard about six hours ago."

She tried to get up. "Well, why didn't you say so? You should go on home and rest."

"That's the problem," he replied, pinning her there. "I don't want to go home. I only stretched this little recon mission out all day so I could be with you."

She had to swallow. Where was that glass of water she'd brought in here? "So you aren't really worried about Mrs. Mitchell?"

"Oh, I'm worried about her. I told you I'd get this man. I intend to do that. But...I'm more worried about you."

"Me?"

"Well, more like how you drive me crazy with that gentle little laugh of yours and the way you pull your hair back with that ridiculously proper silver clasp."

She touched her hair in defense. "It keeps my hair out of my face."

He touched her hair in defiance. "It keeps my hands out of your hair."

The next thing Autumn knew, he had the clasp in one hand and her hair in the other. Somehow, the clasp clattered to the floor while he pulled her up out of the chair, his eyes locking with hers as he lowered his head to kiss her. And while he kissed her, he ran his big, warm hands through her hair, tousling it, tangling it, touching it. Autumn felt as if she'd melted into a puddle of sun-drenched water, felt as if she'd been a leaf falling from a tree, out there floating around on the horizon, just waiting for a spot to land.

She held on to him, sure that she'd never really been kissed before. This feeling encompassed everything her heart was telling her: security, fear, elation, doubts, trust and warnings. Warnings everywhere.

Those warnings caused her to push at his chest and lean back to stare up at him.

His eyes moved over her face again. "You are so pretty. And kissing you is so much fun. And so much hurt."

Autumn couldn't breathe. No one had

ever told her these kinds of things before. She'd tried being fashionable and glamorous, but April and Summer had dibs on those attributes. She'd tried being smart and accomplished, but that only scared men away.

But not this man. This man seemed to see her for herself, and he seemed to enjoy celebrating her true self. He didn't seem threatened or intimidated by her, and he sure wasn't put off by her plain looks or her rigid manners.

In fact, Campbell Dupree was the kind of man who not only echoed her own heart, but reveled in accepting the challenge of…her. His eyes, his kiss, made her heady with delight and paralyzed with fear. Her prayers were being answered, but Autumn had to wonder if she'd asked for the right things. Was wanting this man wrong?

He was standing here in her father's study, his hands trapped in her hair, telling her she was pretty. Kissing her as if she truly was pretty, while he told her it both felt good and hurt at the same time.

"Say something," he said, his head

dipping as he kissed her on the nose with a delicate, delightful peck.

"I'm not used to this."

"To being kissed?" He did it again. "It takes practice, is all."

"No, I mean I'm not used to being the one."

He lifted a dark eyebrow. "The one?"

"The one who's with the man. You know, the one who's kissing the man. I'm usually the one who's giving advice to the one who's kissing the man."

"You're not making any sense."

She touched a hand to his face. "Ah, you see, that's what I'm trying to say. None of this makes any sense."

He danced her around the desk. "Is it so impossible to see yourself as pretty, as attractive, as someone a man could be interested in?"

"Yes, it's impossible. This is impossible. You and me, we're supposed to be professionals. We agreed to be professional. We work together, for my father. And he's already given you the speech. I don't see how—"

"Don't think so much. Just relax and kiss me again. You know what they say— practice makes perfect."

She did kiss him again. Several times. Until the clock in the hallway struck ten and caused her to let go of him and move away to the other side of the room. "I think you'd better go, Campbell."

He looked at her, a reluctant resolve settling over his features. "I know this is confusing. I'm confused. I know all the rules, Autumn. But I can't help what I'm feeling. I can't help breaking some of the rules, because I think you'd be worth it."

"I understand," she replied, bobbing her head as she wrapped her arms against her stomach. "I understand. I'm just not—"

"You're just not ready to accept this," he finished. "Okay, I get it. You kissed me like you're ready, but you still have doubts. I can respect that."

"Campbell, I—"

He held up a hand then started putting files back into his briefcase. "I'm going to get right on hacking into Willard's affairs. I'll trace his latest movements through public records and that sort of thing. We have old addresses on him, but I'm pretty sure he's used different names for different places."

"Okay." She nodded, still holding herself back, her insides coiled into a tight spring, disappointment and embarrassment draining her of any kind of argument. "And I'll dig through county records and probate court. That suggestion one of our sources had about the wills of his previous conquests made sense. If Willard has run through someone else's funds, he's sure to do the same with Betsy's and then he'll start on his next victim."

Campbell nodded, then gave her a long, searching look. "Sounds like we've made some progress, on some things, anyway."

"I'll walk you to the door," she said, then she held up a hand. "On second thought, maybe that's a bad idea."

He nodded. "Probably, because I'd only want to kiss you again."

"Well, good night then," she said, shrinking back against the desk.

"Good night." Then he asked her a question that left her both surprised and touched. And even more confused than she already was. "Will I see you in church in the morning?"

Autumn hadn't thought beyond getting him out the door. "You…go to church?"

"Of course I do," he said. "Does that surprise you?"

"No. Nothing surprises me anymore." She stood silent, then added, "I take that back. You, Campbell. You continue to surprise me. You keep me on my toes, that's for sure."

"Nothing surprising about me, darlin'. I just know a good investment when I see one."

With that, he was gone, his sneakers squeaking on the hardwood floor of the long hallway, their echoes leaving a sure imprint.

Autumn felt as if he'd left a great imprint on her heart, as well.

Chapter Ten

"You and Campbell sure worked hard yesterday," Gayle said at Sunday morning breakfast. "Did you find out everything you needed?"

"We're still gathering information," Autumn said, keeping her eyes averted as she buttered her bagel. She wanted to tell her mother that she'd discovered way more than she ever wanted to know about herself and Campbell. But Autumn figured her mother was asking about Betsy Mitchell and not Autumn's budding love life.

"Are y'all going to be able to get this man?"

Her father's booming question filled

the sunny kitchen like thunder parting a cloud.

Autumn waited for him to sit down at the table. "We plan on doing just that. We're going to dig in a few more places before we go to the authorities."

"Should have done that to begin with, if you ask me," Richard said as he took the cup of coffee his wife offered. "After what you told me last night, it didn't sound as if you two made very much progress. I still think we should just go to the police."

"Daddy, you know why we didn't report this right away," Autumn reminded him. "Mrs. Mitchell didn't want to go that route unless it was absolutely necessary. And after talking to her, I get the feeling she'd forgive Willard if he'd only come back with her money."

"Betsy is a kind soul," Gayle said. "I'm sure she'd rather forgive and forget than be caught up in a scandal. It would hard to face people, I imagine. But she's a strong woman. She'll get through this with grace."

"I just wish she'd let us follow proper

procedures," Richard said, his scowl growing. "I want this man punished."

Gayle patted Richard on the hand and offered him some wheat toast and bacon. "Honey, you know how proud Betsy is. She surely doesn't want everyone at church to hear about this. It's so unfortunate, but people would talk and probably make fun of her. It just wouldn't do to let this get out."

"It might have to get out," Richard countered, his lips jutting in a pout of frustration. "I just can't believe—"

"Don't get your blood pressure up, suga'," Gayle warned. "Autumn and Campbell seem to be on the right track. Why don't we give them a chance to finish what they started?"

"They sure do seem to be spending a lot of time together after hours, too," Richard said into the air, his expression clearly showing his disapproval of the whole situation.

"I'm right here, Daddy," Autumn retorted. "You don't have to pretend I'm not."

"Oh, well, should I pretend I don't have eyes and ears, either?" Richard asked, giving her a sharp look. "I think something else is brewing around here besides your mother's fine coffee. And I think you have a lot to settle up on before this is all over."

Autumn finished her breakfast and got up to beat a hasty retreat. But she turned at the kitchen sink. "I would have thought you'd be glad Campbell and I are getting along. After all, you're the one who put us together."

"Ouch, that hurt worse than the Dallas Cowboys losing in a play-off game," her daddy countered. "You just had to remind me that I hired Campbell without consulting you, right?"

"You're the boss," Autumn said, her back turned as she stared out at the swimming pool. "I'm just trying to do my job."

"Do you like working with Campbell, honey?" Gayle asked. "He seems a likable fellow. Very well-mannered and pleasant."

"He's all of that," Autumn said, still looking outside to where the riot of geraniums in various pots around the pool were sending out their last blooms before winter set in, and still remembering the way Campbell had kissed her last night and caused something inside her heart to bloom as brightly as those flowers. The man was very likable, and very pleasant. "We get along fine at work. We've learned to work around each other."

"You should be working *with* each other," Richard reminded her. "For the good of the company."

"Oh, we're doing that, too," Autumn said, whirling to glare at her father. "As long as things are running smoothly down at Maxwell Financial Group, I guess the rest shouldn't matter. Right?"

Richard threw down his napkin. "Well, don't go and get all testy on me, girl. I want you and Campbell to work well together. I just don't like the fact that you seem to want to spend a lot of extra time together."

"You can't have it both ways, Daddy. I was with Campbell all day yesterday so we could help our client."

"Of course you were, dear," Gayle said, her hand still on her husband's arm, her eyes giving her daughter a calm, warning look. "We understand that." Then she shot her scowling husband the same look. "Don't we, darling?"

"I don't understand much of anything these days," Richard said, still pouting. "But I reckon I just need to stay out of it. For now."

"Good," Autumn said, pivoting to head upstairs. "I'm going to get dressed for church."

"She's going to church with us?" Richard asked in a voice loud enough to echo up the stairs. "Since when has she started going to church with us?"

Autumn heard her mother's smug reply. "Probably since she found out Campbell also goes to our church."

Autumn dressed hastily in a dark green turtleneck and a plaid skirt, then sat down to e-mail her cousins before she took this next step. Things were spiraling out of control and she needed some no-nonsense advice.

Okay, girls, I'm going to church this morning for all the wrong reasons. I should be going to hear the word of God, but I'm mainly going to see Campbell Dupree. I guess I want to see him in that kind of place. You know, a quiet place of reflection. I mean, he's such a ball of energy, it's hard to imagine him sitting still and listening to another human being for an hour. Not to mention singing hymns in church. Just can't picture the man doing that, either. In fact, I can't picture Campbell in church at all, but he keeps telling me he's a true Christian.

I will ask God for direction while I'm there, of course. I know you are both sitting there in open-mouthed surprise right about now. I was the one who missed church on a regular basis back in New York. I was the one who had too much work to do on Sundays actually to take time for the Sabbath. Well, as you are both discovering, things are a tad different in East Texas. Slower, more refined, less harried and urgent. Unless, of course, one is trying to get to church to sit by the man one kissed last night.

Yes, right here in my father's study, of all places. Right here, amid client files and computer printouts, Campbell Dupree kissed me in a way that made me feel as if I'd never truly been kissed before. Are your jaws opened even wider now, or are both of you laughing because you can't see me kissing a man back without hesitation? I did it. I kissed him right back. And girls, I enjoyed it. Do y'all see a pattern here with us? Come home and find love? Is that the plan God had for us all along? Did we have to leave home in order to find home again? Maybe that's what having faith is all about—finding home again. Anyway, I'm off to church. Hope I won't be too distracted by Campbell's gorgeous smile. You should both pray for me. I am really confused. And y'all know I'm never confused. I've always been concise, firm in my goals and sure in my convictions. Campbell has thrown me for a loop. I didn't see this one coming. Need advice ASAP!

Autumn signed off and hurried down the stairs just as her father called up, "We're leaving now."

"I'm here," she said, out of breath as she met her parents in the entryway. "Ready."

But in her heart, she knew she wasn't ready for Campbell so early in the morning and so soon after that kiss. Not at all.

He watched the double doors at the back of the church, his heart doing funny little palpitations that could be a sign of stress or a sign of something much more intense—love.

Campbell turned to stare up at the stained-glass windows behind the altar, thinking he wasn't so sure how this kind of feeling could turn to love. But he'd certainly never felt this way before. His heart hurt and rejoiced at the same time. His brain got all wired and felt rejuvenated each time he thought of Autumn Maxwell. And each time he remembered kissing her, well, there went those palpitations again. Maybe he needed to have a checkup with his doctor next week. Maybe his ulcer was coming back.

Campbell glanced back as the doors swished open and then he saw her. Autumn, wearing a demure high-necked sweater and a proper plaid skirt. Probably had on a set of designer loafers, the kind women wore with little heels that only added to their cuteness. The woman knew how to pick clothes, that was a fact. She always dressed impeccably, whether she was casual or at work.

Work. He really should be concentrating on work. He'd stayed up half the night working the Internet to find clues regarding Willard Watson. It was amazing just how much information was floating around out there, available for all to see and hear. He'd have Willard in custody soon, and all of this would be over.

Then he'd have to get back to work.

But today, he only wanted to enjoy the morning worship service. In his secret heart, he was happy to see Autumn here. She didn't talk much about her beliefs, and yet Campbell knew her parents were solid in their devotion to this church and their community. They lived the life, walked the walk, talked the talk of what having faith was all about. Campbell admired that. He craved that kind of firm, solid commitment. His life had always been a bundle of confusion and chaos. Except for his grandfather's steady hand. Thanks to that, Campbell had a good hold on his own faith.

Up until this morning, Campbell had wondered about Autumn, though. She seemed secure in her faith, based on conversations they'd had about her and her cousins living in New York. And yet, Campbell had sensed a reserve about her, a kind of standing back and watching way of believing. He wondered what it would take to bring Autumn around completely. After all, the woman had to have proof of everything. Maybe she needed proof of God's love for her, too. And maybe Campbell could help in that area.

He stared straight ahead, because he smelled her sweet fragrance before she slid into the seat beside him.

"Hello," she said as the minister and the choir came in to get things started.

"Good morning," Campbell replied, then he turned to face her. "You look great."

"Thanks."

Campbell glanced just beyond Autumn, reached out to shake her mother's hand and was stopped cold by the glaring, burly-bear look Autumn's father was sending him.

"Morning, Mrs. Maxwell," he said, holding Gayle's hand for a couple of seconds. Then he extended a hand toward Richard, which forced Campbell to reach across Autumn, which caused him to inhale the scent of fresh flowers that surrounded her, which in turn caused him to look briefly into her eyes before he felt the strength of her father's hand crushing his own.

"Morning, Campbell," Richard said, the steely warning in his eyes as firm as the steely grip of his hands. "How are you?"

"Good, I'm good, sir," Campbell said, tugging his hand away. He rubbed it to bring back the circulation.

Autumn shot her father a look, then turned to whisper to Campbell. "He's grumpy this morning. Worried about Mrs. Mitchell, I think."

Campbell leaned close as the choir started singing. "I think it's more than that. I think your Daddy doesn't want me around you. He can read me like a book."

"That's silly," she said, her eyes on the choir. "There is nothing to read into this. We've been working. That's all."

"Yes, that's true. But have you forgotten—"

"No, I haven't forgotten anything. And I don't want to talk about it right now."

Campbell saw the blush creeping up her face. "Did your father say—"

"He's said a lot, but we have to work together and we have to find Willard Watson. It might be hard to do that if we try to avoid each other."

Campbell started to speak, but Autumn's mother hushed them both with a finger to her lips. Campbell felt as if he were seven years old again and in trouble as usual.

But then, he *was* in trouble. Big trouble.

He analyzed the situation. He liked his job and he liked his life. But Richard Maxwell could easily take away both. He liked...really liked...Autumn Maxwell, but he wasn't supposed to feel this way about the boss's daughter. He wanted to find the man who'd conned Betsy Mitchell, and Autumn had promised—no, declared—that she wanted to help with that. What could Campbell do to remedy this situation?

He looked up as the preacher welcomed everyone to the service. And he knew what he had to do.

Autumn wouldn't like it. At all.

Her father probably would, however.

Campbell lowered his head as the minister said a prayer. Campbell asked God to give him the direction he needed to accomplish the things he needed to accomplish.

And the strength to walk away once he'd done his job.

"Campbell, want to join us for lunch at the country club?"

Autumn glanced up at her mother's question, hoping at first that Campbell would say yes, then changing that hope to a plea that he'd say no. The look on his face seemed to indicate he was going through the same thought process. As did his answer.

"Ah, no, thanks, Mrs. Maxwell. I've got a lot of work to do back at home."

"Regarding Betsy Mitchell, I hope," Richard added, his hand on his wife's arm. "That is top priority."

"Yes, sir. I intend to get to the bottom of this very soon."

"Want me to help?" Autumn offered, her tone full of defiance as she glanced at her scowling father. She could show him that she was able to separate her personal feelings from her work. Maybe she needed to prove that to herself, too.

"No. I can do this on my own."

She heard Campbell's response, saw the regret in his eyes, and felt an acute disappointment that left her floundering. "Okay. Guess I'll see you in the office tomorrow, then."

"I'll be there," Campbell replied as he waved goodbye and headed off toward his sports car.

"Did he seem a bit put off?" Gayle asked as Richard guided her down the church steps. "Was I just imagining that?"

"He's just preoccupied with Betsy's situation," Richard pointed out. "Poor woman wasn't even in church this morning."

"I'll call her later," Gayle said. "Maybe Autumn and I can ride over and check on her."

"I think that's a good idea," Autumn agreed. "The more we talk with her, the more we can find out. And I know she could use our support right now."

Gayle nodded, then got right back to her original concern. "I just wonder what's on Campbell's mind. I guess he feels as responsible for this happening as your daddy and you." She patted Autumn's arm. "It will all work out. That man won't go unpunished."

Autumn didn't say anything, but she agreed with her mother's assessment of Campbell's behavior. Campbell had definitely changed his tactics, that was for sure. Was it because of her father's dire warning glances all throughout the church service? Or was it because they'd broken all the rules last night with that kiss?

Maybe it was both. Maybe she should step back and not go rushing headlong into a relationship she'd just regret. Campbell could be having second thoughts, or maybe he'd never meant for things between them to go so far so fast.

On the ride to lunch, Autumn thought over things. First, they had to find out about Willard Watson. That had to be done, one way or another. Second, she wasn't about to let Campbell do all the work on that. She was just as responsible as he felt he was, and she needed to clear up this matter so her father wouldn't think the worst of her. Third, she had agreed to work with Campbell, whether she'd felt comfortable with that or not. Wouldn't things get even more sticky if she walked around like a moonstruck teenager instead of a professional who had a job to do?

If Campbell was having second thoughts, then perhaps he was right. Autumn hadn't come home looking for a man. She'd come back to Texas because, well, home was the only place she'd had left. This was her home. This was her life. She couldn't risk messing that up with what could become an impossible situation. Better to concentrate on work and get back to the things that really mattered.

And yet, last night, when Campbell had kissed her, she had felt that *she* mattered. To him. Had it all been a silly mistake, the misunderstandings of a woman who'd never before put finding a man at the top of her list of needs?

I don't need him, she told herself as she watched the brilliance of the fall afternoon passing her by. I don't want to need him.

Then she wondered if her visit to church had backfired on her. Maybe if she'd gone to worship in the right frame of mind, instead of going in hopes of sitting near Campbell, well, maybe then

God would have given her the answers she needed.

Or maybe, in His own way, God had told her exactly how things needed to be.

Chapter Eleven

Campbell pushed back from his desk at Maxwell Financial Group, tracking his thoughts with all the precision of an equity and income fund. He'd just found out some very interesting information about Willard Watson.

"What are you doing?"

He glanced up, his eyes bleary and burning from working at his computer all day, to find Autumn standing in his doorway, her hands on her hips, her eyes flashing like heat lightning. "I'm thinking about going out to the lake, to see how things are coming on my cabin. And I'm thinking I might stop at the Busy Burger and get me some of that good meat loaf they have as the Tuesday special."

He almost asked if she wanted to join him, but refrained just in time. Just in time to see the hurt in her eyes.

She advanced with a kind of golden fury, her brow furrowed, her lips tightly pursed. "No, I mean what do you think you're doing, Campbell?"

Campbell got up, stretched, cracked his knuckles. "I said, I think I'm going out to the lake. It is quitting time, right?"

She nodded, pushed herself toward a chair, her hands gripping the back with an iron-fisted intensity. "Oh, yes, it's quitting time. But I know for a fact that you've been working after hours. Without me."

He winced. In the two days since his revelation in church, he'd tried to stay on the case and stay away from Autumn. Which had made this the longest two days of his life. But he went to bed tired and he worked endlessly to make sure he didn't have time to think about…

Her hair. Her lips. Her smile. Her prim wardrobe.

"Did you hear me?" she asked, standing her ground across from his desk, her big, red mannish tie almost matching the red in her face. "I want to know what's going on with you."

Campbell stretched and winced some more. "I've been doing my job," he said, aggravated that she already knew very well what was going on with him. "Isn't that obvious?"

"Oh, it's very obvious. You've been shut up in here for two whole days and I know for a fact that you've been out on your own, researching Betsy Mitchell's financial crisis. Without me, Campbell."

Campbell hated the hurt in her eyes. "I promised myself I'd take care of this."

"And what about how we agreed to work together? I seem to be the one in charge of consoling Betsy, but I don't have any hopeful news to give her each time I go to visit with her because you're not sharing anything these days. Did you conveniently forget about me?"

He dropped his hands to his side, his gaze holding hers. "There is nothing *con-*

venient about you, darlin'. Trust me on that."

"So you are avoiding me?" she shouted, lifting her hands in the air.

Campbell looked behind Autumn. "Janice, did you need something?"

The secretary looked embarrassed, her gaze shifting from Campbell to Autumn. "I'm leaving now. That is, if it's safe to leave you two here alone?"

Autumn pivoted, her expression reminding Campbell that she was a pure-blooded Maxwell. "What does that mean? Has my father got you spying on us, Janice?"

The sage secretary didn't blink an eye. "Goodness, no, Autumn. I'm talking about how I'm afraid to leave Campbell here with you on account of you might tear his eyes out."

Autumn slumped against the chair, her head down. "I'm sorry, Janice. Things have been a bit tense around here since we found out about Betsy's situation. I didn't mean to take it out on you."

Janice patted her arm. "I don't think

I'm the one you're taking things out on." She eyed Campbell with pity. "But if you don't mind my saying so, I think the best thing you two can do is just go to the police with all the information you have. This man will be long gone if you keep fighting about who gets to do what around here."

Autumn looked down at the floor. "I'm so sorry."

Campbell wanted to fall through the floor.

"You're right, Janice. Shut the door on your way out. Autumn and I have some things to get straight between us."

"Okay, then." Janice gave them a little salute and headed down the hall toward the front of the building.

The silence after her departure was pure and deafening. The whole office seemed to settle into itself while Autumn stood there staring at Campbell.

"What are we going to do?" she finally asked, shrugging. "I shouldn't have made this all about us. This is about helping Betsy. What's happened to us?"

"I don't know," he replied. "I mean, I know what I need to do. And I'm afraid it doesn't include you, Autumn."

The resolved hurt on her face almost did him in. "I see," she said. "So you *are* deliberately avoiding me."

But he could tell she didn't see at all. "It's a bit more complicated than that—"

"You regret kissing me, don't you?" she asked, her eyes so big and vivid he thought surely he'd fall to his knees any minute now.

He couldn't lie to her. "I don't regret anything, except maybe us getting to this point. It was never supposed to be this way between us."

"That's sidestepping the issue, Campbell. We're here now. We can slow down or we can turn back. But…either way, I won't forget that kiss for a very long time."

He threw his hands in the air. "Neither will I. Which is why it can't happen again."

"So you don't like kissing me?"

He let out a soft chuckle, pushed at his

hair. "Oh, yes, I enjoy kissing you so much that I almost made a fatal mistake."

"And what would that be?"

He sank down in his chair and stared up at her. "I don't get involved very often."

"Translate, please?"

"I tend to avoid heavy relationships."

She nodded, crossed her arms as if preparing for battle. "You mean, all of your relationships up until now have been shallow and superficial?"

He had to smile at her blunt way of getting to the burning issues. "Yeah, something like that. Work, Autumn. Work has always been my salvation. I've always been too driven to allow myself to be distracted."

"So I'm a distraction?"

He didn't like the way that question was asked, with that smug little Southern tone. He felt completely uncomfortable underneath the heated scrutiny of her all-encompassing look.

Finally, he sighed and shrugged. "You are, indeed. We both told ourselves this would be a mistake. Your father is on to us, and he's right. I don't need to be messing around with you. And that's what I've been doing."

"Are you telling me this was all part of the game? Part of the setup? Did you kiss me because we were pretending to be a couple and you just got carried away?"

"There was no pretending in that kiss, Autumn."

"So now, because I'm a distraction, because you're afraid to admit your feelings, you're just going to shut me out?"

"I'm not shutting you out. I'm simply…ending things before they go any further, before we get caught up in something that could hurt both of us."

"Too late, buddy. That kiss kind of sealed things with us, don't you think?"

"It was just one kiss."

That remark seemed to slam into her. She pushed away, then leaned back against the doorjamb, shock registering on her face. "I guess you say that to all the women you dump, huh?"

He got up, started toward her, then

stopped. "I'm not dumping you, Autumn. I'm trying to save you."

"I can decide that for myself, thank you very much."

"But—"

"Don't give me that condescending look. We have a job to do and if you're afraid I'll go all sappy and mushy on you and distract you from the day-to-day operations here, or from catching the wayward Willard Watson, then you are sadly mistaken, Campbell Dupree. I can do my job. I've been doing my job for a very long time now. And I've had to deal with a lot of Romeos in all that time. You aren't the first and I'm sure you won't be the last. So you can relax—I don't want a lifetime commitment from you. I don't expect anything beyond what we've already agreed to—to get this mess with Betsy Mitchell's finances cleared up and to get back to our work here. I can handle that. Think you can?"

Campbell put his hands on his desk to steady himself. This had to be the most infuriating woman he'd ever met. If he said no to that pointed question, she'd know he was head over heels for her. If he said yes, she'd only resent him and do her level best to make his life miserable. He was a loser either way. But he knew he had to keep his self-control and do the right thing here. He had to back off and concentrate on his job, on work, on the problem they both wanted solved—no matter how much he wanted to get up and go over there and kiss her silly.

"I can handle it," he said. But that pledge sounded weak, very weak.

"Okay, then. Consider this conversation over. Consider that we never kissed each other and that nothing is going on with us now or ever again."

He had to admire her gumption. "Okay."

"Okay." She came back into the room, her face a beautiful blank canvas. "Now what have you found out about Willard?"

Campbell let out a long sigh. "I can handle this, too, Autumn. In fact, I insist. I don't want you involved."

"I am involved," she retorted as she sat down across from his desk and crossed her legs. "And I'm not leaving until you give me a thorough update. We owe Betsy that, at least."

Campbell got a brief glimpse of pure emotion before her face closed off again. He prayed for God to wipe the image of Autumn's anger and hurt from his mind.

"You should just go on home, Autumn."

She actually laughed. "Don't patronize me. I am not leaving this office until you tell me what you know, Campbell. Just spill it."

"It could get ugly."

"It's already ugly."

Campbell tried to stare her down, but those big amber eyes just held onto his gaze and drenched him in need and longing, pinning him with a rigid determination. "Okay, sweetheart, you win."

"Good." She swung her dainty little foot in triumph.

Campbell tried to swallow. Boy, did he need a drink of water.

Autumn leaned back from her take-out plate. "That was good. Thanks for ordering the food."

"We did miss dinner," Campbell replied, his eyes on the papers in front of him.

If he kept reading the same things over and over, he was going to melt the ink right off those pages, Autumn decided.

"I can't believe that Willard," she said, careful to keep things on an even, businesslike keel. She'd had her say and now things were be…een them were…different. They were back to being courteous and stilted, stoic and concise. Almost downright compatible.

She missed the other way.

But she was determined to show Campbell that she could handle his rejection. Because she had a secret. She knew in her heart that he was only doing this to protect her. Either that, or he was deathly afraid of her father's wrath.

Somehow, she didn't think her father's disapproval would hold Campbell back. But Campbell's own fears and shallow excuses certainly would. Whatever issues he had from his chaotic, unstable childhood had definitely followed him into adulthood. He'd obviously used his career as a tightly built shield from his real feelings and emotions. Autumn wanted to burst through that shield and help him see that what they had discovered in each other could heal all wounds. But that would take time.

Autumn was known for her patience. She could bide her time. She wasn't going anywhere for a good long while. They'd see who could hold out the longest on this standoff. In the meantime, they were getting closer to finding Willard Watson. And that held a little bit of victory, at least.

"So let's review," she said now, glad to have something to concentrate on besides Campbell's cute disheveled hair. "Willard has a history—"

"Willard has a *record*," Campbell interrupted. "Bad checks here and there, traffic tickets never paid and a couple of bogus insurance claims to boot. And we have all of his several names now, too. Will Watts, William Wallace—that's a cute one—Willie Webster and Willard Watson. The man must sound like Elmer Fudd with all those *W* names."

Autumn had to smile at that. "A wegular jack of all twades, that wascally wabbit."

"Yep, a con man down to his fake Italian loafers. But his real Social Security number doesn't jibe with what we know."

"What do you mean?"

"Well, from all the conversations we had with various people who knew Willard, including Betsy herself, he claimed to have been born and raised in Texas. He walked the walk, had the drawl down, even wore expensive cowboy boots hand-tooled down in Austin—probably paid for by some unsuspecting woman—and he *has* lived in several different areas around the state, according to everything I can find on his last known addresses. But his Social Security number doesn't match Texas. The first three digits indicate he comes from Mississippi. Which is why I'm waiting to hear from my sources there."

Autumn nibbled on a cold French fry.

"Very interesting. But what does it mean for us?"

"Well, it means we can finally get the real lowdown on Willard. He might even be heading back to Mississippi as we speak."

Autumn nodded. "Do you think we've waited too long to find him?"

"We'll find him. He'll slip up somewhere. We know he took some of Betsy's credit cards, which we've canceled. But we might have missed one. Betsy couldn't remember all of them. And she said he took out some new ones, probably after he'd raided her bank account. I have a feeling we'll have him cornered soon. Or he might do something really stupid and try to contact Betsy."

Autumn got up to throw away her empty drink cup. "I think we're just spinning our wheels."

"Not really," Campbell said. "I've got feelers out all over the Internet and I've made several phone calls to former clients who are in law enforcement. You know, judges, retired police officers. I have a lot of high-end clients who owe me favors. I think we'll hear something regarding Willard very soon."

Autumn could see the frustration and the sincerity in his eyes. At least he was focused on this. He'd made a commitment to this case. But he couldn't make one to her. Why were men so pigheaded?

"What are you thinking over there?" Campbell asked her, jarring her out of her thoughts.

She tried to be honest. "That you are amazing." Then she leaned over the desk. "I know you're attracted to me, Campbell. And I know that you're backing off because you have this noble streak about as big as Texas. You don't want to hurt me, and you don't want to lose your position here at Maxwell. You're struggling right now, trying to decide which is more important to you—me or my father's company. But in spite of all that, you still want to finish what you started, work-wise, at least."

Enjoying the surprise and chagrin on his face, she turned for the door. She intended to keep him guessing until she had him roped. "I'll see you tomorrow."

He was there, blocking her getaway, before she could make it across the carpet. And suddenly, Autumn felt like the one being roped in.

"Got me all figured, don't you, darlin'?" He stood just outside the door, his hands reaching across to hold on to each side of the door frame. "Got me in this little box that you can admire and analyze with regret, right? And here I thought we'd worked through all of this."

"Campbell, I didn't mean..."

"I know what you meant, Autumn. You think I'll cave, don't you? You think I won't make it through, day after day, being near you? You need to remember I'm a workaholic. I can focus on the numbers—it's all about the money."

She gave him what she hoped was a kind, pitying look. "You *were* a workaholic—you need to remember that. You don't want to bother that pesky ulcer, do you?"

He reached for his stomach, then grimaced. "My ulcer is fine. Probably shouldn't have had those onion rings. But I'm going back to my old bad habits. Things seem to go better that way."

"Don't do that," she said, her heart hurting to see him so determined to avoid his feelings. "I think if we try really hard, we can figure out a way to make this work for both of us."

He still blocked her way, but he stepped closer, interest sparking in his dark eyes. "Oh, you mean you and me, working together?"

"No, I mean you and me, *being* together."

She pushed toward him, causing him to drop his arms. Then she leaned up and kissed him gently on the shadow of his beard stubble. "Good night, Campbell."

He let her by, a kind of hissing breath leaving his system.

Autumn smiled as she got in her car to head home. Smiled and let out a breath of her own. Her hands were trembling; her lips still felt the rough warmth of his skin. She leaned her head on the steering wheel, asking God to help her make the right decisions. Asking God to let her love, just fall in love, for the first time in her life.

Please don't let this be wrong, Lord, she prayed. *I guess You might be getting a real kick out this, sending me such a complicated, difficult man. But if this is a test, I want to pass with flying colors.*

She cranked the car and backed up, and then she caught a glimpse of Campbell standing at the window, looking out at her. She could feel the pull of his eyes, could feel the tug of the struggle going on inside him right now. She felt that same pull, that same struggle.

This sure wasn't going to be easy. But apparently, real love and real commitment weren't supposed to come so easily.

Chapter Twelve

Autumn was halfway home when her cell phone rang.

Grabbing for her purse, she answered on the third ring. "Hello?"

"Is this Autumn Maxwell?"

"Yes," she said, slowing down to pull off the road. "Mrs. Mitchell?" Remembering she'd given the woman her cell number in case Mrs. Mitchell heard from Willard, Autumn's whole system went on high alert. Their recent visits had been pleasant in spite of the subject matter, and Autumn had come to really care about the senior citizen. "Are you all right?"

"Yes, it's me. I...I wanted to tell you

that everything is okay now. You don't need to worry about me anymore."

"What do you mean?" Autumn asked, thinking everything didn't sound okay. Betsy sounded frightened. "Do you want me to come by?"

"No, don't do that." Betsy's voice was shrill and shaky. "Willard and I…have made up. He's back here and…we're going away together."

Autumn held the steering wheel. "Are you sure that's such a good idea, Mrs. Mitchell? The man took a fortune from you—"

"He regrets that. He wants to make it up to me."

Autumn remembered Campbell's words earlier. He'd said Willard might come back. But that could only mean trouble for Betsy. She had to keep the scared woman talking. "Really? How can he do that now?"

She heard an intake of breath. She also heard a voice in the background. "Are you all right, Mrs. Mitchell?"

"I'm…I'm fine, honey. Please just drop

your investigation. I don't want any more trouble. I have to go."

"Wait, don't hang up," Autumn shouted into the phone. "Is Willard there with you now?"

"Why, yes. That's correct."

"Are you afraid, Mrs. Mitchell?"

"That's correct again. I'm not sure of our plans."

Autumn heard a mumbled response and some garbled words. "Mrs. Mitchell, are you there?"

"I was just telling Willard about how nice it was of you to call, dear. But I really need to go now."

Okay, Betsy Mitchell had called her. That made Autumn's radar go up a notch. "Is he holding you against your will?"

"Yes, I think that's a fair statement—"

There was a static-filled silence, then a male voice echoed through the line. "Don't you get it, lady? We're okay here now. Betsy and I are going to be just fine if you and that Dupree fellow will just leave things alone."

"Mr. Watson?" Autumn's hands were

shaking. "Please listen to me. Don't hurt Mrs. Mitchell. She didn't want us to follow up on this, but we felt obligated—"

"It's none of your business," Willard said, his tone sounding shaky and uncertain. "You people just want a piece of her money. Just trying to keep her a happy client. Well, she doesn't need you anymore. I can handle her finances just fine. If you want to keep Betsy safe, you'll just forget about us."

"I can't do that," Autumn said, willing the man to see reason. "Why don't I come over there and we can talk?"

Silence. Then she heard his irritated sigh. "I think that's a fine plan. Maybe if you hear my side of things, we can all get on with our lives, and you and your partner will just leave us alone."

"Okay," Autumn replied. "I'll be right there."

"Fine. Oh, and Miss Maxwell, don't call Dupree or your daddy. You come alone, or…or Betsy and I just might have to head on out of here and you'll never see her again."

The thought of this man hurting an innocent old woman was too much for Autumn to bear. "I won't say a word to anyone. Just don't do anything you'll regret, Mr. Watson. I'm very near Betsy's subdivision. I'll be there in five minutes."

"We're only going to wait for a little while," Willard Watson said on a hiss. "Don't be late."

Autumn hung up, then took a long, calming breath. She should call someone—the police, her father? No, Willard Watson had said to come alone. She might put Betsy in jeopardy if she alerted anyone else. Maybe if she could just calm him down, at least he'd let Betsy go.

Her phone began ringing again, startling Autumn, but when she saw Campbell's number she didn't answer. She was too afraid she'd blurt everything out to him. She had to do this herself. Somehow, she had to help Betsy Mitchell. She wouldn't let that crazy man do anything to hurt Betsy. But Autumn had to admit that she had no idea how to go about helping.

So she did the only thing she could do for now. She prayed—*Please, Lord, help Mrs. Mitchell.*

Campbell frowned as Autumn's phone went to voice message. He hesitated before leaving a message. "Hey, it's me. I'm sorry about…about how I treated you tonight." He held his own phone tightly, trying to find the right words. "I guess…I guess you're right about me. I am afraid. I don't know how to be close to a woman, Autumn. I don't understand. Just give me some time. I don't want you to be upset. I like you when you're smiling at me. See you tomorrow."

Campbell hung up, then looked around the dark offices of Maxwell Financial Group. It was amazing how secure he felt here. He loved the built-in walnut shelves lining the walls, filled with financial tomes. He loved the file room that held all the information on each of their clients. He loved how that same information was readily available on his computer. He loved how the numbers added up, loved

how he could take a small investment and
make it grow over the years. He loved
trying to second-guess the stock market.
It always brought the adrenaline rushing,
this making money. It meant that the
future would be bright, secure, full of
hope. It meant no worries, no troubles,
comfortable retirement, the bills always
being paid. It meant his clients would
never have to worry about where their
next meal was coming from, or where
they'd find the means just to pay the
electric bill. It represented all the things
Campbell had longed for—security, pros-
perity, wealth and means. And a place to
belong.

Now, Campbell saw other ways of
making his own future bright with hope,
and this time, what he saw had nothing to
do with money. He saw big amber eyes
full of need and confusion. He remembered soft lips and a sweet fragrance that
made him think of lush gardens and
blooming flowers. He got an image in his
head of Autumn and him standing on the
wraparound porch of his cabin out on the

lake. He'd hold her hand in his, kiss her slender fingers. They'd laugh and smile and make plans for a family.

A family?

Campbell had to shake his head to clear his mind. Where in the world had that thought come from? He'd never been the settling-down-family-man type. But then, he thought with a bit of bittersweet self-discovery, he'd never met a woman quite like Autumn Maxwell. Just thinking about her made him feel like a better person. Autumn was a paradox. One minute, she was so prim and proper and strictly accountant, it was laughable. The next minute, she was sparring with him, matching him word for word, beating him with yet another great financial equation, or laughing with him at some remark Janice had made.

He liked the way she didn't mind sharing the financial sections of the half-dozen newspapers they received here at the office and how she'd always slip the funny pages in between the financial pages, just so she could hear him chuckle across the hall. On those mornings, she'd come running into his office and grab half of his Danish, grinning at him while he howled over Garfield or nodded over Dilbert. They'd shared this ritual so often, he now sliced his Danish or his bagel in half automatically. He wanted to share everything with her.

Autumn had quickly become a part of his life. It was scary how easily they'd settled into each other's presence. They worked well together, even if things had started off on shaky ground.

It was when they weren't concentrating on work that Campbell got a bad case of cold feet. He'd never ventured this far before. He'd had relationships, but they'd been mostly for show and companionship. This wanting to be around Autumn all the time was more than just companionship. This was something more, something that ran as deep as the waters out on Caddo Lake.

He'd tried to hold back, tried to put some distance between them. But Autumn was too smart to buy his paltry excuses. She knew. She knew that he cared. That made Campbell feel vulnerable and exposed. And yet, he still wanted to make her smile.

And he really just wanted to hear her voice.

Campbell turned off the last of the office lights and locked up, tired down to his bones, confused up to his eyeballs. *I need some guidance here, Lord. I need to know which way to go.*

He couldn't afford to make a mistake with Autumn. He didn't care that he might lose his job. That didn't seem to matter as much as losing a woman who was a good friend, a great work partner and so much more.

"I just couldn't take it anymore."

Autumn sat on the high-backed formal blue sofa in Betsy Mitchell's pristine house, staring across at the man who held a gun on them. The minute she'd arrived here, Willard Watson had hauled her inside and commanded her to sit down next to Betsy. Now Willard was repeatedly explaining why he'd come back to Atlanta to get Betsy.

"So you're tired of running from the law?" Autumn asked, trying to find a way to get through to the man.

"I'm tired of people like you trying to be the law," Willard said, frustration in each word. "Betsy and me had a good relationship. I didn't mean to skip out, honestly."

"But you *did* skip out," Betsy said, her righteous indignation clear as she sat straight-backed on the sofa. "You embarrassed me, Willard. I've never had to hide my affairs before. I've never had a reason to hide anything, until you came along. I can't even look my friends in the eye, I'm so ashamed."

"I didn't want to take your money, Betsy-boo," Willard said, his bifocals slipping down on his big, sweaty nose. "I tried to make us more money at the tracks over in Louisiana."

"But you lost her money," Autumn reminded him. "Besides the fact that stealing is illegal, you had no right to do that."

Betsy stiffened even more. "I detest gambling in any form, Willard. You know that."

"That's why I couldn't tell you," Willard said in a whining voice. "Things just didn't work out the way I'd hoped. I picked the wrong horse."

"Obviously," Betsy retorted. "You wiped out two of my primary savings accounts. And I'm still not sure how many of my charge cards you took."

"I said I was sorry," Willard retorted, the red bow tie at his skinny neck jumping with each word. "If I just had one more chance—"

"I want my money back," Betsy said, her bravado showing now that Autumn was here. "I mean it, Willard."

"Betsy, I don't have your money anymore. It's scattered between here and the horse track."

"You went to the casinos, too, didn't you?" Autumn asked, a dread filling her mind.

"I had to try and get back our funds," Willard said, his beady eyes imploring them to understand.

"*My* funds," Betsy reminded him. Then

she leaned forward. "What are you going to do with us?"

Willard looked from Autumn to Betsy, then he looked at the gun in his hand. "I'm going to take you both with me, just until I can figure out something."

"You can't get away with this," Autumn said, her mind racing ahead. "People know where you are now, Willard. We've already got several people on the lookout for you across the entire Ark-La-Tex."

"Tell *me*," Willard shouted. "That's why I came back. I have my own sources and one of my good friends in Mississippi called me to let me know that Campbell Dupree had been snooping around. How can a CPA also be a detective? Does the man never sleep?"

"No, he's a workaholic," Autumn said, her bitterness all too real, but her pride in Campbell giving her courage. "And he's been trying to track you down for days now. I expect Campbell will hear back from some of his sources any minute now, and then we're going to the authorities."

"You might not make it there," Willard said, waving the gun at them. "I have the upper hand now."

"The upper hand?" Autumn said, anger making her raise her voice. "Do you think taking us hostage will actually help you get out of this mess? You've stolen and lost Betsy's money and you went across state lines with it—I think that's called larceny. I think we can also get you on securities fraud since you broke into her accounts and shifted her funds. And now you can add kidnapping and carrying a concealed weapon to your growing list of crimes. So if I were you, I'd reconsider taking us anywhere. Your best bet is to leave now, while you still have a chance."

Willard got up, held the gun toward Autumn's head. "A chance? A chance? That's all I've ever needed—a chance." He turned to Betsy, the handgun shaking. "You were the best thing that ever happened to me. I kept telling myself now I could finally settle down. I thought the bad stuff would go away. But I was too tempted by all that money. I kept thinking if I could just win us a quick million or so—"

"I had a half million," Betsy wailed. "And my dear George and I worked hard for that money. You don't know the meaning of hard work. You don't understand that there is no quick fix. Oh, Willard, if you'd only tried to overcome your addictions. I would have helped you. I would have sent you to counseling. We could have turned to the church. Everyone would have supported you. But you didn't trust me enough to help you. You just took my money and left me to explain. I will never forgive you."

"I'm too far gone to forgive," Willard said, sitting down on a brocade footstool by the white marble fireplace. Then he looked up. "Did you say a half million?"

Autumn shot Betsy a warning look. "Don't tell him anything else, Mrs. Mitchell."

But Willard wasn't listening. "I only found a hundred grand. I only found one or two money market accounts."

Betsy sighed with relief. "Well, praise God, you didn't get it all!"

Autumn cringed at that lifted thanks. Better to ask God to help them so they wouldn't wind up getting shot.

Willard's eyes grew brighter as a shrewd look masked his face. "I guess I can get it all now, though. You've been holding out on me, Betsy-boo."

"I have other assets," Betsy replied, visibly appalled that she'd let the cat out of the bag. "But I'll die before I let you get to any more of my money."

"That can be arranged," Willard said, his confidence returning now that dollar signs were once again flashing before his eyes. "But first, you need to tell me where that money is hidden."

Autumn was as surprised by Betsy's confession as Willard. Where *had* Mrs. Mitchell been hiding the rest of her assets? Had Campbell and Autumn missed something? Maybe Betsy had more than one broker. Right now, Autumn didn't care. Right now, her only concern was to keep Betsy Mitchell alive, and to keep Willard Watson away from that money.

"You're not going to do that," she said to Willard. "You just told us how much Mrs. Mitchell means to you. I think if you stop right now and turn yourself in, we can both help you in some way. We can help you before you make things much, much worse."

"Can't get much worse," Willard replied. "All I want is enough money to get me out of the country. Just a little nest egg to tide me over."

"Just until you can find another place to gamble it all away," Betsy retorted, her fear replaced with something much more dangerous. Determination. "I refuse to aid your addiction."

Autumn didn't know which one she needed to shake first, Willard or Betsy. But she did know that somehow she had to find a way to get Betsy safely away from Willard Watson before the man did something really stupid—like shoot one of them.

Autumn closed her eyes and prayed.

Please, Lord, send help. Please forgive my stupidity in not calling for help when I had the chance. Please let someone find us. Or at least give me the strength to get all of us through this alive.

When she opened her eyes, she saw Betsy Mitchell's lips moving in her own silent prayer. Willard paced and waved his gun, lost in his own quest.

And to think I was afraid to take a leap of faith, Autumn thought. Now it might be too late to go on that grand adventure, to fall in love, to really live life. She'd come home, hoping to find some sort of peace, some sort of belonging again. Instead, she'd found a difficult man she could easily love, and now she sat trapped by a man who was willing to kill for money. Now she only longed to be able to tell Campbell everything that was in her heart.

If she could only live long enough to see him again.

Chapter Thirteen

Something didn't feel right.

Campbell stood on the porch out at his cabin, taking in the night air and the smell of fresh paint and cedar siding. It was late and he should be getting back to town, but he hated to leave this sanctuary. After leaving Autumn a message, he'd driven out here. He'd just needed a place to get away and think. He'd needed a place that reminded him of his grandfather and home.

And he'd hoped Autumn would call.

Now, however, he couldn't stop this feeling of dread, so he stood watching the lake grow black with shadows as the moonlight cast out a pale, silvery glow over the cypress trees and silent, shining water.

Maybe he was just worried about Autumn. Worried about how he'd tried to push her away. She hadn't answered his call. And Autumn always answered her cell phone. Was she that angry at him? Or was she finally ready to accept that they couldn't be together?

She'd seemed okay, even though things were far from okay between them. They'd managed to get a lot of work done. And although she'd left him with thoughts of how much he needed her, she hadn't seemed upset. More like resigned and willing to bide her time. Even if that were the case, she wouldn't ignore his phone call, would she?

Knowing Autumn, she was probably just giving him some time and space. It would be so like her to recognize his need for both. But Autumn was as practical as the day was long. She would have answered her phone on the supposition that he had information regarding Betsy, if nothing else.

"It just doesn't make any sense," he said, his words echoing out over the quiet cove. Maybe she'd needed some time, too, to reflect and get things straight in her head.

He turned to go back inside to shut everything down. His cell phone rang, causing him to hurry toward the walnut table where he'd left it earlier. He had to acknowledge the way his heart fluttered with hope that it might be Autumn.

"Hello?" he said, ready to reason with her, ready to charm her.

It was her father. "Hey, Campbell. Are you and Autumn still at work?"

Campbell's gut began to twitch with warning and alarm. "No, we left over two hours ago. I'm out at my cabin. She's not home?"

He heard Richard heave a breath. "No, and we're getting kinda worried. She always calls if she's going to be late. She's not answering her cell. Do you have an idea where she might be?"

Campbell pinched his nose with two fingers, telling himself not to go into panic mode. "Maybe she stopped off at a friend's house. She probably can't hear her phone ringing."

"Could be," Richard replied, "but she would have called us if she'd changed her plans. She knows her mama holds dinner until we're all here. Do you think she got a call from a client and went to visit someone?"

Betsy Mitchell. For some reason, her name popped into Campbell's head. "I know she and Mrs. Mitchell have been calling back and forth, and Autumn's visited with her a lot over the last few days. Autumn's tried to reassure her about everything that's happened. Maybe she went by to check on her."

"That could be it," Richard replied, sounding doubtful.

"I could call Betsy and ask," Campbell offered, his mind spinning with all sorts of possibilities.

"Do that for me, would you?" Richard said. "Call me back if you find her. Her mother's worried."

Campbell promised to call them right

back, thinking Gayle wasn't the only one who was worried. He remembered Autumn stressing to Betsy Mitchell to call them if she heard anything from Willard Watson.

What if she had?

And what if Autumn had gone to help Betsy?

That would certainly explain why she wasn't answering her phone. And that would also explain this gut feeling Campbell had right now.

Autumn heard the peal of her cell phone, but she didn't dare move from her spot on the sofa next to Betsy. She glanced over at Willard Watson, thinking the skinny, frightened man looked as tired and frustrated as she was feeling right now.

"Does anyone know you're here?" Willard asked, his eyes going toward her purse and the sound of the ringing phone.

"No, I told you I wouldn't tell anyone." Autumn felt the silence as the phone stopped ringing. "But my parents were expecting me home hours ago. That's probably my father calling."

"Oh, yeah, the great Richard Maxwell. Big man around these parts, isn't he?" Willard said, his tone conversational. "Big money man. All that oil and all those rich clients. He's made a good life for himself."

"He's an honest, hardworking man," Autumn countered. "And he doesn't like it when his family and friends are threatened."

"You trying to tell me he'll come after me?"

"Something like that."

They stared each other down. Then Autumn said, "Just how long do you plan on holding us here, anyway?"

"Shut up," Willard shouted, a hand to his head. "I'm trying to think. Got to think."

Betsy had long ago slumped back on the couch, but her tone of voice was still sharp. "You don't have enough brains to think. If you believe I'll give you the rest of my money without a fight, you are sorely mistaken."

That seemed to set Willard off again. He

lifted his head, then started pacing with excitement, the big handgun hanging in the air as he kept it loosely aimed on them. "I think you're wrong there, Betsy-boo. I just realized I don't need to sit around trying to come up with a plan. I've got the means to get to your money—or somebody's money—right here in front of me."

He grinned down at Autumn. Then he aimed the gun straight at her. "We're going to go to that computer in Betsy's tidy little study and you're going to pull up all of her accounts. Even the ones she hid from me."

"I didn't hide anything," Betsy said. "The money—"

Autumn grabbed her arm, then shot her a warning. "Don't tell him, Mrs. Mitchell. Once he has what he wants, he might just kill both of us."

"Smart girl," Willard said, holding the gun inches from Autumn's face. "But if you tell me what I need to know, and help me get enough money to get out of this miserable little town, I might just let both of you go."

Autumn didn't believe that. Willard was

getting desperate and they were all running out of time. She had the sick feeling that Willard would take them both hostage and demand a lot more money—from her father. But if that was her father trying to call her, Richard Maxwell would soon have an entire posse out hunting for her. And that would be very bad news for one Willard Watson.

Very bad news, indeed.

Campbell threw down his phone in frustration as he put his foot to the pedal of the old Chevy truck and broke the speed limit hurrying toward town. Something was definitely wrong. Autumn wasn't answering her cell at all. He should know. He'd tried her about five times now.

The only explanation had to be that something had happened with Betsy Mitchell. Something bad. Something or someone was keeping Autumn from getting to her phone.

He'd already pulled up Betsy's number on his PDA. Now he was frantically dialing that number. And no one was answering it, either. Hoping Autumn and Betsy had gone somewhere to sit and talk, Campbell kept hitting redial while he headed toward Betsy Mitchell's house.

When his phone rang, he almost lost control of the truck trying to get to it.

"Autumn?"

"No, man, this is Bud."

"Bud?" The friend he'd contacted in Mississippi. Letting out a breath, Campbell asked, "Do you have something for me?"

"Sure do. Willard Watson was seen in the immediate area about two days ago, but he's gone now. Headed back to Texas, from what we can gather."

"Texas? You mean he's on his way back to Atlanta?"

"Seems that way. We asked around and, well, the man lost a lot of money—big-time—at the casinos all the way from Biloxi to Shreveport. He's in a whole peck of trouble. And he's on the run. For the life of me, I don't get why he's running back to Texas. He must be one stupid con man."

"Thanks," Campbell said. "I owe you

one, Bud." He hung up, his stomach aching with the sure knowledge that Autumn and Mrs. Mitchell were in deep trouble. He had to get to Betsy's house.

He prayed he wasn't too late.

Autumn's fingers hit the keys with precision. She'd willed herself to stay calm for Betsy's sake. Willard now had the gun trained on Betsy while he shouted instructions to Autumn. Now I'm a computer hacker, Autumn thought, as she saw Betsy's personal finances flowing across the screen.

"Okay, I'm in," she said to Willard. "This is Mrs. Mitchell's primary account at the bank."

Willard leaned down toward Betsy. "I know about that account, darlin'. What else you got for me?"

Betsy's whole demeanor had changed over the course of the last hour. She looked calm and determined, as if she'd steeled herself against the worst that could happen.

Autumn, however, didn't feel so confident. She glanced over at Betsy, willing the woman just to follow instructions for now.

But Betsy had apparently had enough. "I am not going to give you any more of my hard-earned money, Willard Watson. I trusted you." She gave the look of an ice queen, her nose in the air, her eyebrows lifted. "I loved my husband, and then he died. I was so lonely. And then you came along and made me laugh, made me feel young again. I would have given you anything, anything at all. All you had to do was ask. But you didn't have the decency to do that, did you? You had to steal from me. And all the time, you plied me with pretty words and promises."

Her shrug was so dainty, Autumn would have thought they were having tea out in the back garden. "I don't care about the money. It won't bring back my dear husband, and it certainly won't get me to heaven. So you do whatever you want to do, Willard. If you want to shoot me, then go ahead. I am not afraid of death. And I'm certainly no longer afraid of you."

Her eloquent, impassioned speech

seemed to stop poor Willard in his tracks. He stood there, the gun trembling in his hand, his eyes going wide. "Betsy, I don't want to shoot you. I'm just in a mess here."

"I know that," Betsy said, her hands crossed primly in her lap. "But do it if you must. It will only get me to heaven quicker, while you're left here to get yourself out of this jam."

Willard looked over at Autumn. Seeing no help there, he shifted his beady gaze back to Betsy. "I just need a little more time. I know I'll hit it big one day. C'mon, Betsy, just write me a check or something."

"She can't do that," Autumn pointed out. "You've practically cleaned out her main checking and savings accounts. And most of what I see here is tied up in IRAs and CDs that can't be touched without penalties and a whole lot of questions down at the bank." She shook her head. "We can't just give you a bag of cash tonight, no matter how much you threaten us." Then she turned to Betsy. "Mrs. Mitchell, didn't anyone at the bank alert you to this, or ask you why you were transferring funds recently?"

Betsy slowly shook her head. "I authorized these transactions, Autumn. The bank president was concerned, but I told him I knew what I was doing." Then she glared up at Willard. "He coached me, of course. Told me he knew all about how to invest money. Told me he'd double my savings. I took the money out little by little so it didn't look so bad. I closed out a money market account, and moved some money from my savings to my checking, and told the bank president I was giving it as a gift to a needy friend.

"Which was true at the time, because Willard had me convinced he really needed the money in order to make more money. And I didn't consult Richard. I should have consulted Richard." Then she pointed to Willard. "But he had me convinced I was wasting money paying a financial advisor. I mean, Richard didn't even charge us for any of his services, and I still didn't go to him. This one had me convinced of a lot of things—like marriage and traveling around the world and a life just full of joy and bliss. Next thing I knew, he'd taken over my accounts and left me high and dry."

"That didn't work out the way I'd planned," Willard said, looking contrite for the first time since Autumn had been pulled through the door. "I've tried to explain—"

"There is no explanation for this," Betsy replied in a haughty tone. "There is no excuse for this. You are beneath contempt." She lifted her head in regal disgust, her noble stance like that of a martyr tied to a stake. "So just get it over with. I'm ready to accept the consequences of my stupidity. And I'm ready to get to heaven and my George. He was a real man, and he loved me. *He loved me.*"

Willard looked sad for about a half a second, then he started swinging the gun again. "You know something? I'm hungry and I'm tired. I only came back here to try and reason with you, Betsy. But you are one stubborn woman. I'm not playing games. I want to know where the rest of your assets are—'cause I know you have other accounts now. You were holding out on me all that time. And if you don't get me to some sort of money soon, I'm going to take both of you to someplace where the sun don't shine."

Then he tilted his head toward Autumn. "And I know somebody who'll pay big bucks to get you both back safe and sound. Somebody who can give me a lot more money—without the hassle of having a woman nagging me!" He grinned, rubbed his sweaty neck with his free hand. "Yep, I'm thinking Richard Maxwell would be willing to pay dearly to have his precious daughter back safe and sound."

Betsy rose up. "You wouldn't dare—"

Willard pushed her back down. "Oh, yes, I would."

Autumn stared at the screen, thinking Willard didn't know what he was up against. It was one thing to disgrace a client and take her money, but if he went messing with Richard Maxwell, he'd pay a lot more dearly than any of them.

* * *

Campbell parked his truck down at the church on the corner, just inside the old, stately subdivision where Betsy Mitchell lived. Glad he had on his sneakers, he ran through the midnight-dark streets, careful to avoid waking the sleeping residents. All sorts of horrible scenarios played through his head and his stomach was as churning and choppy as a stormy lake. The faster he ran, the more concerned he became. He had to find Autumn.

When he reached the rambling brick ranch house, the first thing he noticed was that all the drapes and blinds were closed tightly. And one light burned in a corner room. The large, sprawling house seemed so still and foreboding that Campbell wondered if he was just having a bad dream.

"Don't panic," Campbell whispered to himself, thinking it was late and if Betsy was safe and sound and asleep, of course she'd have all the curtains shut. And maybe she'd left a night-light on.

Campbell heaved a breath, then refocused. And that was when he saw Autumn's little sports car sitting partially hidden behind Betsy's big white sedan.

Autumn was in there with Betsy Mitchell. And Campbell felt certain that they were not alone. Dipping into a nearby cluster of lush pink-blossomed camellia bushes, Campbell calmed his breathing and dialed Richard's number.

"I've found Autumn," he said, his voice barely above a whisper.

"Where in the world is that girl?" Richard asked. "And is she all right? Are you all right?"

Campbell slumped against the bushes. "I'm just out of breath. I'm outside Betsy's house and I think Autumn's inside with Betsy. But I think Willard Watson is in there with them."

He heard Richard's sharp intake of breath. "I knew it was a bad idea not to go to the police with this! Now my baby is trapped with that lunatic. I'm calling the police chief right now."

"Good idea," Campbell said, thinking he could probably kiss his job goodbye for getting Autumn involved in this fiasco.

Why had he insisted on being so stubborn and heroic by going after this man on his own? Maybe to show both Richard and Autumn that they could count on him? But right now, that was the least of his worries. "Richard, tell them no sirens. We're going to have to sneak in the back on this one. Watson is probably very agitated, so we don't want to spook him. He might hurt them."

"Well, Custer and cornbread, he's not the only one who's agitated," Richard shouted into the phone and hung up.

Campbell was left with the heavy silence of the disconnected call and a solid fear that he'd finally been reckless one time too many.

And this time, it might cost him much more than he'd ever imagined.

He also realized that he loved Autumn Maxwell. Funny how he'd tried to deny that, how he'd tried to step away from his feelings. He'd been afraid of making that final leap, but now he was afraid he'd never have the chance to tell her that he'd fallen for her.

The realization that he could actually love someone so intensely filled him with an unexplainable bliss, followed now by a cold, solid dread because the one he loved was being threatened. But it also made him a very dangerous man.

He was going into that house to get the woman he loved and the woman she was trying to help out of there. And he didn't even want to think what he might do to Willard Watson once he confronted the man.

But he'd do whatever it took to have Autumn back in his arms and safe.

Chapter Fourteen

Autumn still didn't have a clue as to where Betsy's other finances were hidden. She'd gone through all the accounts and files that Maxwell had been handling for years. Some of them were still secure, but Betsy's two main accounts, her checking and her primary savings accounts, had both been pretty much wiped clean.

"There's nothing here," she told Willard as he hovered nervously nearby. "You took most of what was readily available, I'm afraid. The rest is tied up in stocks and bonds and long-term CDs, which is probably why you weren't able to get to the rest of it. Will you please listen to me and end this right now? I've done all I can do short of robbing the bank."

But Willard Watson wasn't giving up. "She's got some hidden somewhere else, I know. She's a shrewd one, I'm telling you."

"Not shrewd enough," Betsy retorted. "I can't believe I let a cad like you swindle me dry."

Autumn hadn't heard the word *cad* since reading a long historical romance on vacation last summer. But Willard Watson was a cad, that was for sure.

"Keep looking," he said over her shoulder, the fatigue in his shrill command telling her he'd lose patience soon. "If you can't find me some cash real soon, then I'm gonna have to take both you with me and demand money from your daddy. That's a last resort, but it just might be the only answer to all our problems."

"Look," Autumn said, turning to face him. "Mrs. Mitchell has given you the passwords and codes to several of her financial portfolios. You've already hacked into most of them. And the rest of the stocks and bonds are so tied up, it would take an act of Congress to get to them. What's the point of looking any further? We're all tired and this is getting us nowhere. Why don't you either leave and get as far away from Atlanta, Texas, as you possibly can, or just turn yourself in? We can both talk to the authorities, tell them you have a gambling problem. It might make things easier."

"You're crazy if you think I'm going to jail," Willard said, sweat beads popping across his forehead. "I got people all over, including some in the jails and prisons, just waiting to do me bodily harm. I just need to think."

He'd long ago undone the bow tie at his neck. It now hung like wilted gift wrap around his sweat- stained white cotton shirt. "But you're right. This is getting us nowhere. We go to plan B now, I think."

Betsy Mitchell huffed. "You've been threatening us for three hours, Willard. Why don't you admit you don't have the courage to do the right thing—or anything else sensible, for that matter?"

Autumn admired Mrs. Mitchell's bravado, but feared the woman was going to get both of them killed with her smug confidence. Willard was getting more antsy and wily by the minute. "We all agree we just need to end this, right now," she said, her own tone full of impatience. Then she waved a hand at Willard. "I don't think you want to shoot either of us, Willard. Why don't you just put the gun down?"

"No," he said, shaking his head back and forth like a grumpy toddler. "I need something to eat. I need a sandwich and a glass of milk."

"I'll fix you something," Autumn said, getting up from the computer, hoping to win time and maybe find a weapon of her own. "Maybe you'll see reason on a full stomach."

Betsy let out a snort of disgust. "He can starve, for all I care."

Autumn eyed the gun, then leaned over to Mrs. Mitchell. "Work with me here, please. I'm trying to save your life."

Betsy looked chagrined for a minute, then wiped at the skirt of her teal-colored dress. "I reckon I could spare him a last meal."

That really added to Willard's agitation. "Don't push it, Betsy-boo. I don't like your attitude. I thought you really cared about me."

"I did," she said quietly, all smugness gone. "That was a fatal mistake."

Willard ran a hand over his wispy hair, then looked over at Autumn. "I'm in a big fix here, ain't I?"

"The worst kind of fix," Autumn replied. "Let's go in the kitchen and see what we can find for you to eat. Then maybe we can figure out what to do."

"I can take you hostage after I eat," Willard said, his tone conversational and downright cheerful as he lifted Betsy from her seat and shoved her in front of him, the gun trained on Autumn. "I think that's the only way out of this."

Autumn didn't intend to go anywhere with this man. She only hoped that by now her father had someone out looking for her. And she really hoped that Richard Maxwell wouldn't rush in with guns blazing and get himself hurt in the process. She thought of Campbell and lifted up a prayer for him. At least he was safe.

Unless her worried father had called him, looking for her. That scenario sent new fears coursing through her already frazzled system.

She checked Betsy's expression, thinking the woman was a rock under pressure. Somehow, Betsy Mitchell had gone from a victim to a survivor all in the course of a few hours. She wondered how the woman had done it, and then she saw the slight movement of Betsy's lips.

Betsy Mitchell was praying her way through this crisis. As she dug through the refrigerator, looking for sandwich meat and mustard—and a possible weapon—Autumn decided to follow Betsy's lead.

Campbell stubbed his foot against a pine-tree root centered in the middle of Betsy Mitchell's sprawling backyard, and grimaced in silent pain. He'd managed to sneak through the squeaky wrought-iron gate by opening it slowly, creak by creak. Expecting a SWAT team or some other such heroic rescue squad any minute now, Campbell curbed the macho need to rush in and save his woman. And his client.

Saving them might be out for the moment, but he did need to see with his own eyes that Autumn was all right. If she wasn't, then he'd become a one-man SWAT team. But he had to be careful that his actions didn't do any more damage to Autumn and Betsy.

So now he found himself crouched up beside the big bay window at the back of the house. No sooner had Campbell positioned himself where he could see into the dark kitchen than a light popped on and in walked Autumn, Betsy and Willard Watson. And Willard had what looked like a Saturday-night special aimed at them.

Well, the gun wasn't so much aimed as it was being held and waved. Willard looked haggard and disheveled. Betsy looked prim and proper. And Autumn looked mad and impatient.

She had that endearingly irritated look that Campbell knew so well. It didn't mean good things for the man with the gun.

Campbell watched, fascinated in spite of the pounding tremor of his heart, as Autumn argued back and forth with the erratic Willard Watson. And all the while, the woman Campbell loved worked on creating a massive sandwich.

For the man who was holding her captive.

Campbell had to smile. He'd planned on rushing in to save the day. But Autumn apparently had the situation under control. In her usual sensible way, she had done a quick analysis to decipher the problem. Feed the criminal, calm him down enough to make him see reason, then persuade him to turn his life around.

It was so…Autumn.

Campbell's heart swelled to new proportions of love and need as he watched Autumn slicing tomatoes and breaking lettuce into precise, crisp pieces. He couldn't hear everything she was saying to Willard, but the man seemed to be listening as she read him the riot act.

Campbell decided the best thing he could do at this point was to watch and pray. So he did just that.

But he'd been so intent on watching Autumn, and Willard had been so intent on arguing with her, that neither of them had been paying much attention to Betsy Mitchell.

At about the same time Autumn slid a glass of milk and a stacked ham and cheese toward Willard, Betsy Mitchell stood up and grabbed a nearby cast-iron skillet off the top of the stove. Willard let go of the menacing gun long enough to reach for the sandwich. Campbell looked on in horror, as if watching a slow-motion movie, while Betsy raised the skillet and pinged Willard squarely on his ruddy, balding head.

Willard's hands flailed out, one knocking over the glass of milk, the other shoving the gun even farther away and,

Campbell noted thankfully, out of reach. With a look of total surprise and acute agony, he went down for the count, then passed out cold on the tile floor.

Autumn and Betsy grabbed each other in a tight, confident hug, then stared down at him as if he were a nasty cockroach.

Through the relief and tears of victory, Autumn heard a distinct pounding. It must be her heart. She couldn't believe what Betsy Mitchell had just done. She didn't know why she hadn't thought of that herself. She'd considered using the butter knife, but never the skillet.

Willard now lay in a puddle of two-per-cent milk, with a bulging red knot on the top of his wispy-haired head.

"Is he…dead?" Betsy asked, her tone indicating she was completely over Willard Watson and his wayward ways.

"I don't know," Autumn said, her voice sounding faraway and hollow to her own ears. And there went that pounding sound again.

Glancing up, she realized the pounding

was coming from the window in the breakfast room. And the person doing the pounding was Campbell Dupree.

He stopped pounding, his eyes locking with hers as the unspoken message of love and relief in his eyes held her there. He'd come to rescue them.

Her hero.

She'd never seen a more welcome, beautiful sight.

"Don't move," she told Betsy, gently lifting the woman away so she could rush to open the back door and fall into Campbell's arms.

He had her before she'd finished turning the bolt.

"Are you all right?"

"Yes," she managed to say, tears mingling with the giggles coming from deep inside her frazzled system. The scent of his aftershave, the rasp of his beard shadow, the feel of being alive and in his arms was too much for her. She felt the tears bubbling over in her throat and her eyes. "I'm okay, really."

Campbell pulled her back to stare at her,

his hands touching her face to wipe away tears as he scrutinized every pore of her skin. "He didn't hurt you?"

"No, no. Just a standoff. And none of us willing to concede."

"I kind of noticed that," Campbell said, still holding her as he pulled her back into the room. Then he glanced over at Betsy. "Are you okay, Mrs. Mitchell?"

"I will be," Betsy said, her hands clasped at her stomach, "as soon as we can remove this piece of vermin from my presence. I never want to see him again, dead or alive."

Campbell bent down to touch three fingers to Willard's pulse. "He's alive. But he won't be bothering you any more. I called 911—"

Before he'd even finished, two police officers rushed inside the open back door, their guns drawn as they issued orders for everyone to raise their hands in the air.

All three standing people complied. Then there was a moan from the floor and Willard valiantly held up one hand, too.

"Is this the culprit?" one of the officers asked, glancing around for an answer.

"Yes, sir, that's your man," Betsy said, stepping back to give the officers room. "He stole money from me, then held me hostage, then tried to steal even more money from me—and…he upset my friend here."

"I'm fine," Autumn said, waving one hand. "Honestly, he mostly just made idle threats. But he did hold a gun on us. And he did steal money from Mrs. Mitchell."

"We'll need your statements," one officer said as the other one bent down to check on Willard. After verifying that Willard was alive, he called in the paramedics. "I think he's gonna have a pretty nasty concussion. We'll check him out, put a guard on his door at the hospital if he has to stay overnight. Then we'll get on with sending him away for a long time."

"Don't let him loose," Betsy admonished. "He might be stupid, but he's also very dangerous."

"We won't," the young officer told Betsy, an indulgent smile on his face. He bent on one knee and proceeded to read Willard his rights.

Then another ruckus started at the front of the house. There was the sound of loud arguing, then feet stomping down the long hallway, followed by a roaring male voice calling out Autumn's name.

Autumn gave Campbell a tired, tear-stained smile. "That would be my father."

"Are you sure you're all right, honey?"

Richard had asked Autumn this question several times over the course of the evening.

"I'm fine, Daddy, really," she said as they all sat around the huge den of the Maxwell home. Campbell sat on a high brass-backed chair by the long kitchen island across the room. Betsy Mitchell sat on the sofa near Gayle, who'd insisted Betsy come and spend the rest of the night with them. Richard perched on the edge of his favorite leather armchair, his brow furrowed in worry.

They'd had some decaf, since Gayle had told them they were too hyped up for real coffee. Then she'd forced them to eat some crackers and cheese. Now, they were getting ready to go off to bed. Autumn stifled a yawn and said, "I'm just glad to be here with you all, safe and sound."

"Me, too," Betsy said, her smile full of appreciation. "You should be very proud of your daughter, Richard. She was a real trooper tonight."

"I am proud," Richard replied, beaming with relief. "And very thankful that you two are safe and that scoundrel Willard Watson is going to jail." Then he leaned forward. "But Betsy, I have one question. Where in the world *is* the rest of your money?"

Betsy waved a hand in the air, then fingered her pearls. "As Autumn explained, I have a lot tied up in stocks and bonds. But even though you took excellent care of us, Richard, I'm afraid George had a stubborn streak as wide and deep as Lake Palestine. He hid a lot of cash underneath the floor of the attic, in a fireproof safe."

Richard let out a hoot of laughter. "You mean all this time, you and George have been squirreling away money in your attic, and it was right over ol' Willard's head all night long?"

Betsy nodded, then gave him a prim smile. "Last count, I reckon I had around two hundred and fifty thousand dollars in cash, mostly in twenties, of course."

"Of course," Richard replied. He glanced over at Autumn. "If that don't beat all. George always was a tough one. I had to strong-arm him even to get him to consider investment strategies."

Betsy gave them all a long stare. "I think maybe I need to do something with that extra cash. Autumn, will you help me to sort through things?"

"I'd be glad to, Miss Betsy," Autumn replied. Then she glanced at Campbell. "I think we can take care of your assets, and I promise we will watch over all of your funds very closely from now on. Right, Campbell?"

Campbell grunted, nodded, but stayed quiet, his gaze centered on a colorful ceramic rooster decorating the center of the island.

Autumn looked over at Campbell. Other than insisting he drive her home, he'd been awfully quiet since they'd gotten here a little while ago. He'd been watchful while Autumn and Betsy had given their statements to the police. He'd been silent when Richard had ranted about Autumn getting caught up in this kind of danger in the first place. And he'd been downright morose now that they were all winding down.

He just sat there, looking at her every now and then, as if he had so many things to say and no way at all of saying them.

Then he hopped off the stool. "I'd better get going."

Richard got up, too, followed by Gayle and Betsy.

Autumn decided she couldn't just let him walk out the door, so she hurried over to Campbell. "I'll walk you out."

Richard held up a hand. "Autumn, you need to go on to bed and get some rest—"

Gayle gave her husband a tug on the arm, followed by a pointed look. Betsy gave him that same look. Richard tried to speak, then shrugged in defeat, his brow furrowed again as he looked from his wife to their guest.

"Good night," he said, turning to head up the back stairs with a definite stomp.

Gayle kissed Autumn. Betsy gave her a silent hug. Then they both followed Richard, leaving Autumn and Campbell alone as they strolled slowly toward the front of the house.

Autumn opened the front door, but Campbell held it, allowing her to exit first. They made it to the front steps before Campbell turned to face her.

"I'm sorry."

She stared across at him, saw through the glow of moonlight the shadow of regret and fear on his face.

"For what?"

"For putting you in that kind of danger. I should have listened to Richard. I should have let the authorities handle this."

Autumn felt the clutch of love for this man deep inside her heart. It hurt and it healed all at the same time. "It wasn't your fault, Campbell. I went to Betsy's on my own, without calling for help. That's my fault."

He touched a hand to her cheek. "Only because you put Betsy's safety first. You weren't thinking about yourself."

"But I should have been more careful," Autumn said, reaching up to clasp his hand. "I'm just glad it's over finally. I'll be more careful from now on, I promise."

"I'm the one who should be more careful," Campbell replied, pulling his hand away. "I've always been a risk taker, you know. I've always liked that feeling I get, living on the edge. I've surfed in Hawaii, just for the thrill of that big wave chasing me. I've skied down dangerous mountains, just to prove a boy from a swamp in Louisiana could do it. I've sailed yachts and driven fast cars, just to say I've won the race."

He pulled her in his arms, his eyes wide and dark as he looked down at her. "But nothing has ever scared me the way seeing you tonight in that kitchen with a gun being held on you did. I've never felt this way before, Autumn. I would never have forgiven myself if something had happened to you."

He kissed her, his lips soft and reassuring on hers, his touch telling her that he loved her, that he was willing to take yet one more risk. Autumn felt all the worries and fears of this night lifting away like dark clouds clearing for the sun. Everything was going to be all right, she told herself as she kissed him.

So she told him that. "It's okay now. We're together and we're safe. It's over."

Then he lifted his head, touched a finger to her cheek and said, "Yes, and that's why I have to resign my position at Maxwell and leave Atlanta. And the sooner, the better."

Chapter Fifteen

~❧~

Autumn stood there, stunned and hurt, watching as Campbell bolted down the steps and headed for his Chevy.

Then she bolted right after him. "Just hold on, Campbell Dupree. If you think you can kiss me like that and then just walk away, you are sorely mistaken."

He turned, his hand on the door latch. "Autumn, please don't make this any harder—"

"Oh, please!" She rounded on him, throwing her hands up. "Don't give me that line. I know you love me. I can feel it each time you look at me. And I sure felt it in that kiss." She pointed her finger at his chest. "I saw it when you were standing at Betsy's window, pounding to be let in." Then she leaned close, her hands over her heart. "I'm letting you in, Campbell. I'm letting you in."

She reached up to kiss him, willing him to let go and just love her. But she felt him stiffen, felt him slide behind that mask of self-control and sheer determination that made him such a financial wizard. She should know how that felt. She'd been that same way all of her life, too. They'd both put numbers and spreadsheets way ahead of emotions and true happiness, simply because that was more comfortable, more safe, than opening up their hearts.

So she backed up, stared up at him. "Okay, I know you want to go back to being the professional that you claim to be, so you can't feel the things you're feeling right now. I know you're not ready to admit anything. And I think that after what happened tonight, you're so afraid of losing that control, you can't take the next step. If it helps at all, I feel the same way."

He lowered his head. "I don't know

how to take the next step. I don't want to mess up."

She nodded, stepped back again, her hands palms up in front of her. "Well, *I* know how now. I've learned how, from being around you, Campbell. You said you were always willing to take risks. I'm the complete opposite. My cousins had to do some heavy persuading to get me to move to New York with them. I was so afraid to leave Texas. I was terrified to let go of all the things I held dear. I felt safe and solid here, secure. I'd always had this dream of taking over my father's company after college. But they told me I needed to get out there and live, really live, before I made that decision. My parents encouraged me and supported me, even though I'm sure they were hurting inside. But they let me go, and I'm so glad they did. Because now, being home means even more to me than it ever did before."

She held her hands clasped at her chin, almost as if in prayer. "It means more to me now because you mean so much to me. And because I'm needed here to help good people like Betsy. You've shown me how to take those risks, how to step out of my safety net and just let go.

"Did you ever stop to think that if we hadn't intervened and tried to help Betsy, things might have gotten even worse for her? She might have kept all of this a secret, out of embarrassment and shame. And Willard might have gotten to her tonight because she wouldn't have had the courage to call us.

"Don't you see? This isn't your fault. You didn't do anything wrong. We helped a nice woman get justice. And yes, it was risky, it was scary, but we did okay together. We survived. Don't use that as an excuse to give up on us."

He stood poised as if ready to take flight. For one minute, Autumn thought she'd convinced him. But then the mask of resolve fell back across his face. "I can't do it, Autumn. I just can't do this. Tell your father I'll be gone by the end of the week."

Then he got in his truck and left her standing there in the moonlight.

* * *

Autumn sat at the breakfast table, unaware of her mother and father sitting across from her. It had been a week since Campbell had told her he was leaving. And it had been the hardest week of her life. Seeing him at work each day, watching him slowly pack away his books and files—that was just too much to bear. But even more unbearable was the way she'd catch him looking at her, his eyes dark with some sort of torment, his expression somber and full of resolve. They'd pass each other in the hallway, but Autumn had stopped rushing into his office each morning to hand him the funnies. And she no longer took the other half of his Danish. He no longer brought her fresh coffee. It was as if Campbell had shut himself down, his only purpose to make sure all his clients were taken care of, just until he could leave.

So Autumn sat, staring at the *Wall Street Journal,* not seeing the article about how much the stock market had fallen this week. Not caring about the Dow Jones or the economy.

"Looks like rain," Richard said as he ruffled the paper. "Could use some rain."

"It'll probably turn cold after that," Gayle said. "Fall is sure in the air. Think I'll go buy some more mums for the front garden."

"Good idea," Richard replied. "And while you're at it, why don't you buy some of those spirit-lifting plants for Autumn. You know, the ones that grow like weeds and cure all broken hearts."

"I don't know what kind—" Gayle stopped, stared across at Autumn. "I don't think our nursery carries those, darling."

"Well, they sure should," Richard said, throwing down the paper. Then he leaned toward Autumn. "Hey, you with the big, sad eyes. Eat some of that bagel. 'Bout time to get moving. Don't want to be late for work."

Autumn looked up, startled to see both her parents giving her pity-filled looks. "I'm fine. I'm not hungry. And I'm not going to work today."

Gayle caved in, grabbing Autumn's hand. "Oh, honey, is it because Campbell's leaving today?"

Autumn gritted her teeth to stop the pain. "No, it has nothing to do with that. It's just that I've been working night and day since I came home. I need a day off." She looked at her mother, tears welling in her eyes. "Let's go shopping." Then she burst into tears.

Helpless, her father got up in a hurry. "I'll go in today, honey. I'll see to it that Campbell Dupree is good and gone. I told that boy not to hurt you and now he's gone and done that very thing. Maybe I'll just blacken both his eyes and get it over with."

"Don't do that," Gayle warned. "Just let him go. I'm sure he has his reasons—"

"He loves me," Autumn blurted out. "That's his reason."

"Oh, my," Gayle said, looking from Autumn to her husband. "Oh, my."

"Well, is the man stone-blind and stupid, too?" Richard asked, throwing his hands up in the air. "How can he love you and treat you this way? And how can he just up and quit? I don't like a quitter. I didn't peg that boy for one, I sure tell you."

"He's not quitting," Autumn said through sniffs. "He's just getting out while he can. Campbell has a serious commitment problem—when it comes to women, that is."

"I'll show him commitment," Richard said, stomping toward the door.

"Don't do anything crazy," Gayle called. "That will only make things worse. Remember, a kind word turns away wrath."

"I don't have any kind words," Richard stated, his expression clearly full of anger and justifiable wrath.

Autumn got up and rushed to her father. "Daddy, I'll be all right. Honestly. It's just that—"

Richard took her into his arms. "It's just that you love him back, don't you, sweet pea?"

Autumn nodded against the comfort of her father's cotton shirt. "Yes."

Richard held her back, his big hands on her arms. "Well, we have us a problem then, don't we?"

"It's my problem, Daddy. I have to be the one to fix it."

"Oh, and how you gonna go about doing that?"

I'm still calculating," Autumn said. "I have to analyze the situation and figure out a plan."

"That's my girl," Richard said, grinning. "Got to earn some interest on that investment, huh, sweetheart?"

"Something like that," Autumn said. "I was kind of hoping for the big payoff." She sighed, sniffed back tears. "So, please, Daddy, just stay out of it. If you want to go and tell Campbell bye and good luck, that's fine. But don't fight this battle for me. I have to deal with Campbell my own way."

"Okey-dokey," Richard said, kissing her on the nose, his eyes full of doubt. "But you just say the word—"

"I know, you'll be happy to bash his head in. No, thanks."

Richard left, his deep scowl telling Autumn that he might not be able to resist doing just that.

She turned back to her mother then. "I tried not to fall in love with him, Mama."

"I know, honey," Gayle replied. "But we don't always get to pick who we fall for—sometimes it's just written in the stars." She smiled, glancing toward the door. "That's how it was with your father and me. One look, and I was lost and in love."

Autumn sank down on her chair. "How do y'all make it work? You've been married for so long and I've seen you two fight, but you've never been cruel to each other. You've never denied each other. You two have such a sweet, abiding love. Even after all this time. I wish I could get Campbell just to *admit* that he loves me. You two make it look so easy, but it's not, is it?"

Gayle patted her hand. "Of course it's not, honey. Your father and I have had our share of ups and downs. But we not only love each other, we also respect each other. And we've always put the Lord first. We turn to Him when things get tricky."

"I turned to Him the night Betsy and I

were in trouble," Autumn said. "Miss Betsy prayed the whole time, and so did I. And then I looked up and there was Campbell, standing at the window. I knew then that I loved him. I think that's when he realized he felt the same about me."

"And it scared him silly, didn't it?" Gayle asked, pouring them both another cup of coffee. Her amused expression didn't help Autumn's blue mood.

"Apparently. I don't think he's very good at intimacy. At opening up to his feelings. He has issues left over from his childhood. Being poor and having a mother who didn't give him very much maternal attention has left him confused, I think."

"Men are mules," Gayle said on a pragmatic note. "Sometimes we have to give them a good swift push to get them up that hill."

"I did push," Autumn said. "But I won't beg and I won't force Campbell into something he's not ready for."

"So you're going to hide away here until he's gone?"

"I'm going to give him the space he needs, until he finds it in his heart to come back to me. He will, Mama. I have to believe that."

"Then I'm gonna believe it right along with you, honey. And I'm gonna pray it so."

"Thanks," Autumn said. "I think I'll go sit out by the pool for a while."

"Then we can do the town," Gayle said. "Go to lunch, get our nails done, and do some serious power-shopping."

"That sounds great."

Autumn watched as her mother hurried off to get dressed. Then she slumped onto the table, her head in her hands, her heart aching as she thought about Campbell packing up and leaving today. She wouldn't be there to witness it, but she couldn't help the tears that started flowing all over again at the thought of it.

She took her laptop with her out to the pool, and immediately poured out her heart in an e-mail to her cousins.

I never dreamed I'd fall in love, back here in Atlanta, of all places. Daddy brought Campbell here, knowing I'd get all bent out of shape about it. If I didn't know better, I'd think Daddy cooked up the whole thing just to get me to come back and work at Maxwell. I mean, he didn't even know I'd be out of work and somehow it all fell right into place. But Campbell needs Maxwell more than I do, I think. And yet, he's giving it up to protect me. Mighty noble of him, since it's so obvious he's just trying to protect himself.

Now I know how you both must have felt when you fell in love. It doesn't come all tied up in a pretty package, does it? Love hurts, it's hard to grasp, and yet, it's the best feeling I've ever had. I want what you both have now. I had to come all this way, back home, to realize that. Now, having had that kind of joy, I don't think I can go back. I don't know how I'm going to manage without Campbell, but I guess for now, I have to do just that. I'm going on faith that Campbell will find his way back to me.

She signed off, then sat soaking up the cool morning air and drifted into a soft, tired sleep to dream of marriage and children and love and laughter—while the tears dried on her face.

Campbell finished putting the last of his financial books into a box, then looked around his office. It was as if he'd never been here at all, he thought, the bitterness curling inside his stomach and causing his ulcer to radiate with pain.

"You are an idiot."

He turned to find Richard Maxwell blocking the doorway, his solidly built frame as formidable and firm as the conviction in Campbell's heart.

"Yes, I am that," Campbell admitted, hoping Richard would slug him good and proper. "I should have listened to your advice, but I didn't."

"You hurt her," Richard said, stomping into the room. "If you hadn't already resigned, I'd fire you so quick your empty head would be spinning."

"My head *is* spinning," Campbell

replied, "but if you want to punch me, go ahead."

"You'd like that, wouldn't you?" Richard retorted. "You'd like someone to rub salt into your wounds. Or maybe knock that chip off your shoulder?"

Campbell whirled, his knuckles going white as he leaned across the desk. "I deserve it, don't I? I did the one thing I told myself not to do. I fell for the boss's daughter."

"Yeah," Richard said, advancing into the room to the desk, his own hands fisted on the calendar pad. "Yeah, you did. But I never figured you for a coward, Campbell. You talk the talk, try to walk the walk of some kind of grand adventurer. The rugged, hardworking, hard-living financier. The man who's not afraid to take on anything or anyone. Except a sweet little hundred-and-twenty-pound woman who's head over heels in love with you. That little girl of mine sure has you running scared."

"Yes, she does," Campbell said, angry and beaten. "I *am* scared, Richard. I've never felt this way before. It's so…" He slumped down in his chair, wiped a hand down his face. "It's so amazing. And scary. And…she leaves me breathless. I've never been breathless before."

"That's my girl," Richard said, sitting down himself. "I want to protect her from you, but, son, the woman loves you. She loves you. And she's willing to wait until you have the good sense to come around. You won't find that kind of commitment in every female CPA in Texas."

"There will never be another CPA for me," Campbell told him. "Autumn is the only woman for me."

Richard slapped a palm on the desk. "Well, turkey and dressing, man, why can't you just tell her that and be done with it?"

"You know, you're the third person to tell me that today."

Richard looked surprised. "Who else would take the time to harass your sorry self?"

Campbell lifted an eyebrow. "Well, I got it with both barrels from Janice first thing this morning. Then I had a nice visit from Betsy Mitchell. She brought oatmeal cookies—which were delicious, by the way—then gave me a sound reckoning on being yellow-bellied and cowardly. Then she called Janice back in and they both gave me a we-love-you-but speech. My ears are still burning from that encounter."

Richard chuckled. "If both Janice and Betsy said it, then it must be so, son. They make a powerful duo. What are you waiting for?"

Campbell thought about that. What was he so afraid of? Hadn't he climbed mountains just to become the man he was today? Wouldn't his grandfather tell him to run toward the light, instead of turning away from its warmth? He lowered his head, closed his eyes and prayed. And in that prayer, he finally understood what life was all about. It required taking the real risk of loving someone. It required going on faith, and not knowing for sure what the outcome would be. It required believing in hope and happy endings.

Richard remained silent for once, seemingly lost in his own hopes and prayers.

Campbell finally lifted his head, then smiled and nodded, tears welling in his eyes. "It's a long-term investment, isn't it, sir?"

"With the best dividends imaginable," Richard replied. "Big yields, plenty of bonuses and a lifetime of growth."

Campbell got up, reached over to shake Richard's hand. "Thank you for not hitting me."

"It ain't over yet," Richard warned him. "Just think, if this deal takes, I'll be your daddy-in-law."

Campbell's smile was wry. "That should make things very interesting."

Richard got up and grinned again. "Count on it."

Autumn felt a flutter across her cheek. She must still be dreaming. She could see Campbell's face through the haze of her slumber.

Then she sat straight up, looked around. Saw him sitting there on a chair pulled up beside her chaise lounge. And his hand was reaching out to touch her face.

This was no dream.

"Hi," he said, his expression full of resolve and hope.

"Oh, hi," she said, her heart full of longing and hope. "What are you doing here?"

"I had to see you—"

"To say goodbye?" She got up, spun around so hard she hit her shin on the chair. With a hop of pain and a grimace, she pointed a finger at him. "I won't say goodbye, Campbell. I'm not going to tell you goodbye. Because I'm not giving up on you. On us." Then she turned away, waving a hand. "So just go, go and be gone. I can't—I won't watch you leave."

Before he could open his mouth to speak, she whirled back and pushed at him. "But I will be here waiting, Campbell. Waiting and watching, hoping and praying that you'll come to your senses and—"

He grabbed her, hauling her to him. "Could you hush up for just a second, please? I have something to say and I don't want to lose my nerve."

"Oh, you have some nerve, you sure do," she said, anger making her snap out the words. "But—"

"But," he said, pulling her close, "I need to kiss you right now."

So he did. Long and hard and with a confidence and thoroughness that left no doubt in her mind. Until Autumn realized that he wasn't walking away. Yet. She lifted her head to stare up at him. "A long kiss goodbye?"

"Nope, a long kiss hello. I'm knocking again, Autumn. Will you let me in?"

"That depends," she said, seeing the spark of amusement and assurance in his eyes. "Are you coming or going?"

"I'm staying," he said. "I love you." He shrugged, then let out a shaky chuckle. "Wow, that wasn't as hard as I thought it would be."

"Who made you say that?" she asked, looking around, pretty sure she saw a curtain fall away in the kitchen. "Did my daddy whip up on you and make you come here?"

"No. He gave me a good man-to-man talking-to, but I was already beginning to see the light even before he talked to me. It seems both Janice and Betsy want me to stick around, too. They paid me a visit right before your father. And they both said, in unison, kinda, and I quote, 'You'd better go and find Autumn and tell her you love her, or we're gonna hog-tie you and take you to her.' I believed them, but I still wasn't sure, until your daddy told me that I was an idiot. He was right, as always. I am an idiot. But I'm also crazy in love with …u. So…here I am."

Autumn's heart started singing with a sure joy. "You mean, for good?"

"Of course. At least for the next fifty years or so—with guaranteed annuities and compound interest. Lots of compound interest."

She finally smiled. "That does sound long-term."

"Very long-term." He kissed her again.

"What do you say? Are you willing to invest in a reformed reckless idiot?"

Autumn touched a hand to his wayward hair. "I think you're worth the risk."

She kissed him again, letting her heart pour out into the kiss. He held her close, kissed her hair, her eyes, her lips.

"I'm scared," he whispered. "But I have to admit, you thrill me more than any adventure I've ever been on."

"I love you," Autumn said. "I really do, Campbell."

"I love you, too," he said. Then he leaned back to stroke her hair away from her face. "So, how are we getting to the wedding—Corvette or Harley? Maybe we could take one to the chapel and one on our long honeymoon at an undisclosed location."

She grinned. "Maybe the Chevy. It seems to be your best ride."

"Good idea. That ol' truck sure likes you."

Then she slapped at his arm. "Is that your way of proposing, asking me to ride in one of your fancy cars?"

He dropped down on one knee. "I don't have a ring yet, but yes, I'm proposing. And please don't turn me down, because I'm pretty sure that your parents and Betsy and Janice are all in the house right now, watching us. Make it look good, okay?"

She did. She nodded, jumped up and down, shouted "Yes" at the top of her lungs, then she kissed him again.

The back door came open as her parents and the others spilled out, laughing and clapping.

"Oh, how very special," Gayle said, tears streaming down her face. "We're going to have a wedding!"

"I can't believe he actually did it," Janice added, her smile wry.

"I had complete faith," Betsy chirped, her hands clasped together in delight.

"This is good," Richard called. "I might just let you live after all."

Campbell waved to them, breathed an exaggerated sigh of relief, then pulled Autumn back into his arms.

"I love this family," he said, grinning.

Epilogue

"You look a little green around the gills," Richard Maxwell told his future son-in-law. "Nervous, Campbell?"

Campbell nodded. "Just a bit. I mean, the whole Maxwell clan is in this church, just waiting for me to fall on my face."

"Naw, son. They're waiting to watch you marry my daughter," Richard said, slapping him on his shoulder. "Now that is going to be a sight to see. You know, April and Summer have been fussing over her since the day they found out she was spoken for."

"I know," Campbell said, his nerves jumbling together like a twisted barbed-wire fence. "I've heard all about the details. Big church wedding, fancy candlelight reception back at your lovely and historical home. Nothing like a Christmas wedding."

"Nothing like marrying the woman you love," Richard replied. "And speaking of that woman, I'm going to find her and give her a kiss." He turned at the door. "And remember—"

"I'll remember," Campbell said. "I will always take care of her, Richard. You have my word on that. But you need to remember, your daughter is the one who takes care of me. I'd be lost without her."

"Good. I think y'all are going to have a blessed, long life together. I'm sure glad I didn't have to whip up on you."

Campbell waited as Richard shut the door, then turned to face himself in the mirror. He intended to do just that—have a long and blessed life with Autumn. And he knew that life would be rich and full because of Autumn's persistence and integrity. She'd already convinced him to make amends with his mother. And his mother was here today, at his wedding. At long last, she'd shown up. And she seemed as proud of this union as anyone.

Campbell closed his eyes in a prayer of thanks.

"At long last, I'm safe."

Autumn turned from the church window to smile at her cousins. "You both look so pretty in green velvet."

"And you look pretty in white," Summer quipped, grinning. "Honestly, Autumn, you've never looked lovelier."

"Brides always look pretty," April said, making last-minute adjustments to Autumn's hair. "Of course, it does help to have a designer dress from Satire, I reckon."

"And the best fashion tips from two very knowledgeable and chic cousins," Summer added.

April smiled. "All of that aside, Autumn, you are just glowing. I think you'd look pretty in a flour sack. Maybe because you are in love with a very handsome man."

"I owe it all to you two," Autumn told them. "I couldn't have done this without you both."

They stood together, arm in arm, smiling.

"We've all changed over the last year, haven't we?" April said, her dark hair glistening in the early dusk. "Who would have thought that I'd be back with Reed, or that Summer would soon be getting married, too."

"Sorry I trumped you," Autumn said, "but Campbell was in a big hurry."

"It's okay," Summer replied, patting her arm. "Mack and I needed to wait a while. It's been the best thing for Michael. I don't mind giving Mack and his son some time to get to know each other. I'll have them both for a very long time. And now, I'm thinking a spring wedding with all the trimmings."

"You've sure mellowed," Autumn said, laughing.

"Well, April's right. You're glowing," Summer replied, tears in her eyes. "I'm so glad you're in love, sugar."

"And I'm expecting," April blurted,

tears running down her face. "Reed and I are going to have a baby. I tried to keep it a secret, but I wanted you both to be the first to know. Reed is beaming, so it will be hard to stay quiet."

"Ohhh," Summer and Autumn said in unison.

"That's wonderful," Autumn told her cousin. "I'm so happy for all of us."

"We have angels watching over us," April said, looking toward heaven.

"We sure do. Strong, determined Maxwell angels."

"Home-town angels," Summer added, sniffing tears away.

Autumn grinned. "And we all know that Maxwell angels have the biggest hearts. Texas-sized hearts."

They all laughed, then heard a knock on the door.

"It's time, girls," Richard said.

April rushed to the door, her long green gown rustling.

Richard came in, took a look at Autumn, then teared up. "I don't know what to say, honey."

She smoothed a hand over her long-sleeved white velvet wedding dress. "Say you'll walk me down the aisle."

"Reluctantly," Richard told her. "But willingly. He loves you, and I think he's a good man, even though he is wearing sneakers with his tux. But giving you away to him brings me comfort."

"That brings me comfort, too," Autumn said, laughing.

They waited as her bridesmaids left to do their duty.

Then Autumn and her father entered the hallway to the sound of wedding music. And when she started up the aisle and saw Campbell standing there waiting for her, she knew that these steps toward him were much more than just a leap of faith.

They were taking her on a path to the kind of love she'd always dreamed of having, the kind of love that was as big as all of Texas, and just a unpredictable.

* * * * *

Dear Reader,

It's sometimes hard to just go on faith. We're only human, after all. We have so many questions. Sometimes, we think we need concrete proof. Sometimes, we just hope and pray. Autumn had to see things in order to understand them, even though she'd been raised in a faithful family. Campbell was more of a risk taker. He went out and conquered his fears through faith. He believed that no matter what, God was in control. But Campbell had to learn that lesson the hard way. Together, Autumn and Campbell made a nice balance of logical thinking and good, clean fun.

I hope that you will take a leap of faith and let God become the one in control of your life. You can control your destiny as long as you allow God to be in the details. We can hope and pray, while we work hard and make our dreams become reality. Sometimes it is fun to just take that leap and see where we land! As long as we trust in God, we will always be all right.

Until next time, may the angels watch over you, always.

Lenora Worth

QUESTIONS FOR DISCUSSION

1) Why did Autumn come back to Texas? Should she have stayed in New York alone?

2) What made Campbell change so much? Why was it important to him that Autumn understand this?

3) How does this book deal with family and death? Did it help you to understand these things in your own life?

4) Do you think Autumn wanted what her cousins had found—love, family, happiness? Or did she just come home because she was lonely? Why do you say that?

5) How did the competitiveness between Campbell and Autumn fuel their attraction to each other? Do you think it's wise for couples to work together, day in and day out? Why or why not?

6) How did Autumn's parents' solid marriage help her to see that it was okay to fall in love?

7) What did Campbell's recklessness teach Autumn?

8) What did Autumn's cautious nature show Campbell?

9) How did Autumn's close relationship with her cousins help her to find love and happiness?

10) Did reading this series help you with your own family? Why do you think it's important to put family first?

eHARLEQUIN.com

The Ultimate Destination for Women's Fiction

The eHarlequin.com online community is *the* place to share opinions, thoughts and feelings!

- Joining the community is easy, fun and **FREE!**

- Connect with **other romance fans** on our message boards.

- Meet your **favorite authors** without leaving home!

- **Share opinions** on books, movies, celebrities…and *more!*

Here's what our members say:

"I love the friendly and helpful atmosphere filled with support and humor."
—Texanna (eHarlequin.com member)

"Is this the place for me, or what? There is nothing I love more than 'talking' books, especially with fellow readers who are reading the same ones I am."
—Jo Ann (eHarlequin.com member)

Join today by visiting
www.eHarlequin.com!

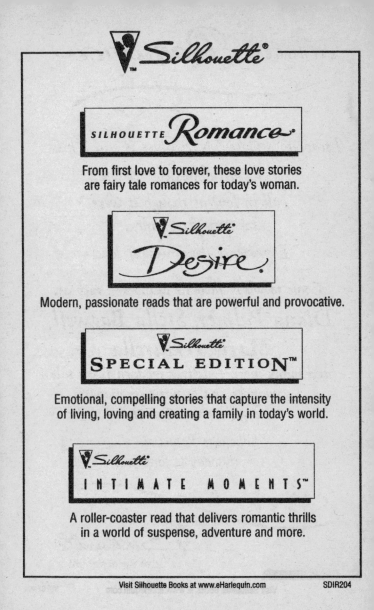

SILHOUETTE Romance

From first love to forever, these love stories
are fairy tale romances for today's woman.

Silhouette Desire

Modern, passionate reads that are powerful and provocative.

Silhouette SPECIAL EDITION™

Emotional, compelling stories that capture the intensity
of living, loving and creating a family in today's world.

Silhouette INTIMATE MOMENTS™

A roller-coaster read that delivers romantic thrills
in a world of suspense, adventure and more.

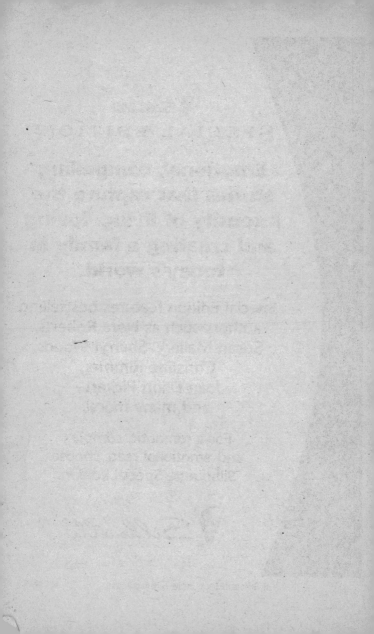